Michael Power was born in 1933 in Pietermaritzburg, Natal, and educated at St Aidan's in Grahamstown, the University of Natal and Oxford University, where he took an honours degree in jurisprudence. From 1962 he worked in the public relations department of a large South African corporation, based in Johannesburg. There in 1964 he was associated with the founding of Blue Crane Books in order to publish the works of Credo Mutwa. His own writing career began in 1962 with the publication by Cassell of his first novel, *Holiday*, which was followed by *A Gathering of Golden Angels* a year later. He also then contributed short stories to several outlets, such as *The Cornhill Magazine* and *New South African Writing*, and worked on *The South African Tatler*.

His third novel, *Shadow Game*, appeared from Michael Joseph in London pseudonymously (as by 'Laurence Eben') in 1972, followed by a Panther paperback two years later. Both printings were embargoed and banned in South Africa. This edition is the first to be available to readers – and under his own name – in his own country. Currently he lives in retirement in his hometown.

Margaret Smith in *The Sunday Times*, Johannesburg (19 July 1962):
'A startling first novel called *Holiday*, by a 29-year-old South African, Michael Power, has caused a stir in the wealthy Natal social circle it describes. Many people have been shocked by the young author's approach to human conflicts. Despite their disapproval they have rushed to buy the book. In ten days most Durban bookshops have sold out their stocks and have placed large repeat orders.'

ill Edgson in *The Star* (23 August 1963):
'By the end of *A Gathering of Golden Angels* its leading character has notably matured. Much the same can be said of Michael Power's writing.'

Paddy Kitchen in *The Scotsman*, Edinburgh (21 October 1972):
'For a writer to present in his first novel the combined theme of apartheid and homosexuality with no awkwardness or excess emotionalism is quite a feat. But in *Shadow Game* Laurence Eben looks at South Africa with a sensitive eye and creates a totally

believable, non-embarrassing love affair between Ray, a young white man, and Victor, a slightly older African. The end must be tragic; no other, given the real-life circumstances in that country, would have seemed right. But before that, Laurence Eben has depicted the characters of a small homosexual clique, trying to live civilised, humane lives, with real delicacy and humour.'

Virginia Osborne in *The Sydney Morning Herald* (19 May 1973):
'It is a fine and sensitively written book which pulls no punches. It has a very factual quality about it – Mr Eben is not trying to involve the reader by using their heartstrings as a harp. I was most impressed by this book.'

Stephen Gray (in 2008):
'In 1973, shortly after its first publication, like so many South Africans abroad before me – Douglas Blackburn, Beatrice Hastings, Stephen Black, Herman Charles Bosman – I resorted to the echoing British Museum Reading Room to bone up on what was not available at home owing to censorship proscriptions. I was wearing a mac, hat and tinted glasses, in order not to be identified as ferreting after our much prohibited mystery-man, Laurence Eben. I was deeply shocked when a copy of *Shadow Game* arrived on the green leather desk, with its cover of intertwined South African black and white lovers, contravening the Immorality Act. The fact that they were both male as well had me silenced for the rest of my trip.'

For further details consult the Michael Power entry on the website of KZN Literary Tourism at http://www.literarytourism.co.za.

SHADOW GAME

Michael Power

PENGUIN BOOKS

PENGUIN BOOKS

Published by the Penguin Group
Penguin Books (South Africa) (Pty) Ltd, 24 Sturdee Avenue, Rosebank,
Johannesburg 2196, South Africa
Penguin Group (USA) Inc, 375 Hudson Street, New York, New York 10014,
USA
Penguin Group (Canada), 90 Eglinton Avenue East, Suite 700, Toronto,
Ontario, Canada M4P 2Y3 (a division of Pearson Penguin Canada Inc)
Penguin Books Ltd, 80 Strand, London WC2R 0RL, England
Penguin Ireland, 25 St Stephen's Green, Dublin 2, Ireland (a division of
Penguin Books Ltd)
Penguin Group (Australia), 250 Camberwell Road, Camberwell, Victoria 3124,
Australia (a division of Pearson Australia Group Pty Ltd)
Penguin Books India Pvt Ltd, 11 Community Centre, Panchsheel Park,
New Delhi – 110 017, India
Penguin Group (NZ), 67 Apollo Drive, Mairangi Bay, Auckland 1310,
New Zealand (a division of Pearson New Zealand Ltd)

Penguin Books (South Africa) (Pty) Ltd, Registered Offices:
24 Sturdee Avenue, Rosebank, Johannesburg 2196, South Africa

www.penguinbooks.co.za

First published by Michael Joseph, London, 1972
This edition published by Penguin Books (South Africa) (Pty) Ltd, 2008
Copyright © Michael Power 1972, 2008

ISBN 978-0-143-18556-7

Typeset by CJH Design in 10/12.5 pt Palatino
Cover design: Flame Design
Printed and bound by Paarl Print, Cape Town

Studio portrait of the author by John Heydenrych (1962)

Michael Power in retirement (2008)

For Jane, my sister

1

While he was laughing he was saying, 'There it goes. Parys. We're over the State border, they can't catch us now.'

'Parys, Orange Free State.'

'Vrystaat!'

'Wait till you see the other Parys. They call it Paris over there.'

'Nonsense, man. Me? And you? Paris? Those are fancy dreams and you know it.'

'One of the things I can't stand about you is your pessimism.'

He said, 'I've told you before. Dream for your own sake, leave me out. You'll trip yourself up if you won't listen to me.'

'I hate your pessimism.' My foot sank towards the floor.

'Steady on, man.'

'Oh for Christ's sake,' and I took a quick look at his face staring straight ahead as though willing another road sign to rear up next to the slimy navy blue tarmac that flowed mile after mile through the beige mealie fields towards the town we were heading for.

'That was a corner and you were warned it was.'

'The next corner is after Kroonstad. So just relax for the next twenty miles. Light me a cigarette.'

'Full of cheek, hey?'

I held up two fingers for the cigarette.

'Okay, get us to the horizon. Verdoemde Voortrekker.'

'There you go again, like all South Africans. Always pinning on labels. You see the label first, afterwards the person. Thanks.' The tip of the cigarette was creased from the pressure of his powerful lips. I put it between my own and at last drew on it. After a few seconds the smoke went towards the windshield, then was whipped through the little side window into the fast bright air.

'You white people,' he said, 'started the practice.' Behind his light tone one caught the coldness. He was dead against me, if only for the second in which he spoke.

'You black people seem to have fallen into it pretty easily.'

He gave a distant little sarcastic laugh, swerving his face towards the window. 'Subject people always pick up the most attractive traits of the people in command.'

'How disgusting. I never heard of such a weak-kneed attitude. Subject people should say to hell with your labels and your shitty refrigerators and canopied beds and perfectly hideous garden furniture, then rise up and grab their knives and slit the throats of all those perfumed bitches in their canopied beds. Just you give some serious thought to this idea.'

'H-e-y.'

The wavy drawn-out syllable and long whistle that followed it filled the car and I glanced at him, not quite sure of developments. He was grinning at me rather feverishly. The short thickly packed lashes round his shiny black and white eyes were straight and silky, without the least crimp in them. It was on account of this, when I first met him, that the thought occurred to me: You have Indian blood in you, did you know that?

'H-e-y. How about us getting a knife?'

'Whose throat have you got in mind?'

'Anyone's. As long as it's white.'

The car we were riding in was a chocolate and olive-green Ford with fittings to match. It wasn't his, or mine, of course. The Organisation, the huge bumbling monster of a company that I worked for in those days, kept a pool of cars that you drew on when you had a job to do at one of the mines or factories that were dotted about all over South Africa, in most cases in the dismal waterless areas in which precious metals are invariably found.

2

Victor Butele and I were on our way to a gold mining town in the Orange Free State. Of the four mines in the town our company controlled three and later that day one of them was being officially opened by a cabinet minister. My job was in the public relations department, I wrote and designed house journals for the mines.

Victor Butele was a radio announcer and I had persuaded my boss that he should come along to cover the ceremony. Good idea, we want the Bantu to know what we're doing for their people on our mines, he said. I thought so, I said.

Victor lit me another cigarette and I accelerated very unobtrusively. The broken brown mealie sticks and thorn bushes and fiery winter grass flashed across my eyes as the first mine headgears, like toys, came into sight far away. I was twenty-one and knew almost nothing about life and I was incredibly happy.

'We'll go straight to the mine and, when everything's over, I'll meet you at the main gate. I'll check in at the guest house, then I'll take you to the goddam compound where they have a room for you. Afterwards we can go for a drive or something.'

It was always like this for us. There were almost no places where we could be together: a web of laws had been spun to keep us apart. If we had not continually used our inventiveness to put up smokescreens between ourselves and other people, we would hardly have seen each other at all. Like all black people in South Africa, Victor had always been obliged to lie. Quite soon I picked up the habit, though I lied less efficiently than he did. Strangely enough, we felt safest in the place most potentially dangerous for us, the house we shared together. Behind its walls we laid a maze of false trails and this calmed us somehow.

No matter how you tried to simplify it in your mind, life for us could not be worked out in ordinary terms. All that we wanted to be able to do, really, was what other people did, yet without those other people being aware that we were doing so.

The likelihood of our being able to pull this off, however, was scarcely possible. Nevertheless we persisted in our illusion. No other method of living seemed bearable.

'I'll show you the main gate, don't worry,' I added.

How stiff and chilly it was in the car all of a sudden. Having left Johannesburg in fits of laughter, we had been driving all on our own for three hours with the world shut out. Now people were marching up and down the street and a car loping in the opposite direction was hooting aggressively at nothing in particular and I felt there were eyes everywhere scrutinising us.

'It's a model town, it was delivered straight from the drawing board on to the bare veld. I mean, it takes guts, doesn't it, to make something quite so ugly? Here's the gate,' I said.

We drove through; the palms of my hands left blurs of sweat on the steering wheel.

'I'll park near the plant, where the ceremony is, and you can meet the compound manager who's going to look after you. He'll give you lunch afterwards somewhere and the minute they start bringing round liqueurs I'll leave the club and come back here and meet you at the gate, say, about three.'

I locked the car and we followed the crowds across the gravel to the arch of flags at the plant entrance and a few minutes later Victor was being led away to a side door by the compound manager, a bellowing man with warts tucked into the side of his nose, who often explained at great length that his rapport with blacks had the soundest of all possible roots, a childhood spent cheek by jowl with his father's farm workers and their offspring way back in the good old summertime.

One of my colleagues swept up with a sheaf of commemorative brochures. 'So you've arrived at last. Did you drive here in reverse?'

'That's not what my passenger was complaining about.'

'Who did you bring down?'

'Some radio type.'

'Next time we'll upgrade you to Reuters. You're opening car

4

doors for VIPs now.'

I stood under the flags with the silky winter sunshine flapping against my face. The next minute the chairman, a subtly shy little mole who mistrusted flunkies and his PR department simultaneously, skipped out of his Rolls before anyone could get near him, but his wife curled her lip briefly at me as I drew her and her sables towards the triumphal arch.

Inside the plant the crowd was hunched on severely raked stands facing the dais and the sinister grey-green rolling mills. The sunshine on one's retina slowly folded away in the gloom. When the bandmaster signalled, a chord was sounded and everyone shot up for the national anthem.

Ons sal antwoord op jou roepstem,
Ons sal offer wat jy vra,
Ons sal lewe, ons sal sterwe,
Ons vir jou, Suid-Afrika.

Behind me somewhere, in a little sliver of the stands separated from the rest, Victor must by now be unwinding his recording equipment, switching it on. I didn't move a muscle, I bolted myself in. I had done this so often when on my own in crowded streets and in places where we could not be together that the process had become second nature. In a split second I could re-create his presence with such a shimmer to it that when, later, he walked into our room, for the first moment or two the man himself seemed to be somebody else altogether.

Ladies and gentlemen, a voice kept on repeating. The cabinet minister's trousers were like laundry bags, the shoulders of his jacket pitched and tossed. He was a stumpy little figure with strangely workmanlike hands which he constantly pushed into the air in front of him. He told us, in many different ways, that we were God's people. He told us God had showered gifts on us, including gold and Christianity. Several hours later, it seemed, he said it was for him a very deep privilege to be invited here today and he was honoured to declare this mine,

Oranje Vrystaat Geluk mine …

With palm upturned, the chairman directed the cabinet minister towards the button. The rolling mills sighed, presently coughed a little. Their roar shook the whole plant and everywhere people rocked against one another and clapped inaudibly and pressed their fingers into their ears. Against my better judgement I was carried away by it all, in much the same way as by an attacking production number in a musical film which, taken as a whole, amounts to nothing but showmanship.

Slowly we all steered outside into the sunshine and people were spinning here and there to get to their cars. I ran towards my friends, the Stanfords.

As usual Dick was pulling abstractedly at a hair on the hood of his nose. He was a director of the company, so we would not have been friends in the normal course of events. How we had met was through an African music group of which he was the chairman and for which I used to help backstage. At a rehearsal one night he had learned that I worked for his company, a long way down at the bottom of the public relations ladder. It seemed to please him that young people in the Organisation were making contact across the race-line. He believed in 'contact'; one often heard him expressing this view in a low cool voice. It was in his presence that Victor and I had met, and he approved of what he saw, which was merely what he was permitted to see, the surface and no more. Part of him was a loner, the other part of course was a financier.

His wife Margaret, who was much younger than him, said, 'Imagine having to miss a lecture on Giacometti to come and listen to that little monster.'

Dick held up a forefinger. 'Now, Meg, wait till you're in the car.'

'We. Us. Our. Who exactly are these fortunate people he kept babbling on about?'

I couldn't help laughing at Margaret's furious green eyes. She yanked at her outlandish cape and glared at Dick.

'The volk. Who else?' I said.

'Volk. The most appalling word in any language.'

Margaret gave a short neigh as she cantered ahead across the gravel.

Dick followed more sedately, he always did. 'You handed Victor over in one piece?'

'Whether he's still in one piece I won't know till three o'clock. The compound manager is giving him lunch à la Bantu.'

'Victor's a sensible enough chap not to let silly little absurdities get him down.'

'It must be hard going for him all the same.'

'He doesn't show it, for which one admires him.'

Even with Dick, of course, far and away my closest older friend, I had to keep a check on myself repeatedly. So I merely said, 'Yes, I suppose so.'

'You'll be back in town tomorrow?'

'Yes, late. Victor's interviews will take the whole morning.'

We came across Margaret next to the car staring dreamily at the outline of shaft headgears and weird pipes that bent this way and that across the wall of a smelter. Established artists claimed she had no individual talent whatsoever, that she had arbitrarily cast herself in a role which reflected her temperament, or so she believed. Nevertheless her eccentricity in a strait-laced city, and her dependence on kindred spirits to keep her going, kept many of us on her side.

'Don't forget,' she said, 'Saturday night. Our opera friends from the Cape. Will Victor be free, or tied up with that disgraceful radio station that doesn't pay him a living wage?'

'No idea. I'll ask him.'

'Tell him we expect him. And give him a lift, or see that someone else does.'

'Yes,' I said.

'See you Saturday. About eight.'

They sailed off among all the other cars while a bumpy little wind suddenly carried a wave of gritty dust through the air.

I raced out of the clubhouse at five to three, flung my notebook on the back seat and drove towards the mine. The gin and the rosé and the Van der Hum hardly affected me at all. I had discovered by then that, while drinking, one of the ways of riding liquor was to keep yourself alive to some other sensation that engrossed you far more intensely than the liquor did. I was young enough to feel terribly elated at having scored some small victory over circumstances. And so I started yelling some pop song or other at the windshield. I saw him, it seemed, from miles off. Say if I have a blowout. Or the back axle snaps. Hasn't it ever happened that a steering wheel simply comes away in one's hands?

'On the dot,' he said. His face filled the window.

He said, 'Did chairman Langenfelder and Mrs Langenfelder let you go with good grace?'

'Mrs Langenfelder looked like she wanted to go too … back to Cap d'Ail, anywhere where they don't have cabinet ministers.'

'Doesn't she care for South Africa?'

'Neither of them do, why should they?'

'Good question.'

'Climb in,' I said.

'The door's locked.'

'But the window's open.'

'Jesus.'

Victor pulled up the knob. I was paralysed, all I could do was keep my hands on the wheel, my foot on the brake. Victor threw himself back in the seat. Only a few days before, a visitor had said the only really alive faces in our city streets were black faces. I couldn't take my eyes off Victor's face, no matter how I tried. Black skin isn't just black skin full stop, which is the lesson infused into us as children. We gobbled it up without a second's thought. Naturally enough, a black skin responds to states of mind in precisely the same way as any other skin. When Victor was on top of the world the vibrancy of his skin was enough to put your eyes out. But possibly all it amounts to is that this perfectly obvious phenomenon has significance only for those white people who happen to find themselves under the thumb of their black lovers.

'Now I can smell the Van der Hum on you.'

'Thank Christ you don't smell of kaffir beer.'

'They gave us real beer. Castle. What do you know?'

We drove off down the dead straight monumental road that, if you go on and on, leads you to Bloemfontein, a city where railway lines endlessly converge below a fort on a cliff left over from a war long ago.

'And to eat?'

'A sort of stew and jelly and custard. You know how it goes.'

'I mean, everyone behaved properly?'

'There were a couple of indunas from the compound, one haughty, the other terrified, a reporter from *Drum*, a photographer from *World*. The compound manager's dumb. But he had pink Lux in the gents.'

'As long as no one tried to – '

'Ray, you know how I've told you: don't *worry*.'

'Okay, okay, sorry.' I picked up a little speed. At the company guest house I ran inside with my case and was shown to a cabbage rose of a room looking out on to wintry peach trees, all wiry and delicate. I dumped the case on the bed and the housekeeper asked me to put it on a riempie stool and gave me my key. No, I wouldn't be in to dinner, I said, and ran outside again.

We set off through the half-hatched town to another mine, where there was a room for Victor. I took him into a gaunt office to introduce him to the hostel superintendent. From the door of the office I watched them growing smaller and smaller as they reached the end of a raw brick corridor, then vanished round the corner. This was the first time we had been away from home together, I was boiling over with resentment and wanted to bash my crunched up fists into whatever face appeared within reach. Instead I obeyed the rules we had set ourselves and made my mind a blank.

When Victor and the hostel superintendent came into view again I went and sat in the car to think of something funny to say. Strangely enough, there was no need of this. We were so pleased to see each other again that we simply picked up the threads from where we had left off, as though nothing had imposed itself in between.

The sun disappeared early and we were tired of driving around. I went into a Greek café where there was a delicatessen counter and bought rollmops and salami and dill pickles and pumpernickel and anything else that caught my eye. In the boot of the car I had packed a basket of brandy, wine and glasses and our dry ice container, named Minorca, our lucky island, because our landlord had let us his house while he went off to live there for a year.

A sad hush lay over the town now that the shops had closed. Blank spaces, where one day buildings would appear, looked like missing teeth in the harsh semicircle of the civic centre. The car streamed soundlessly down the main street under motionless puddles of ice-blue electric light. There was not a soul about and Victor said, 'You know what? I'm keen to get home, and you?'

'Ja, it's better there.'

'But it's good for us to get away now and then, I suppose.'

'Depends how far you want to get away.'

'Well. Malaga. Not further than Malaga. To start with.'

'I don't know.'

'Geoff's said it more than once. His house in Malaga is empty most of the year.'

'Where exactly is this damn Malaga anyway?'

'There's a map at home. Why the hell don't you look it up yourself?'

'And after that? After Malaga?'

'I don't know either. I mean, give me time to think, can't you. But there's something about Malaga that seems okay. You've seen Geoff's slides. That marvellous Alameda and that beat-up Moorish fort at the top of the hill. Don't you like the look of the house too? All those vines and shutters and everything a bit crumbly. The hotel across the road is the Miramar. It would be our local.'

'But how can we take off without a plan, without – '

'I'm not saying we are taking off, I'm not even – '

'Tell me what you are saying, then maybe I'll understand you.'

We passed the last houses and the road shot through dark veld behind the furthest mine to the dams which I had written countless stories about in our journals. The civil engineers were obsessed by them and very proud of them. Millions of gallons of brack water were pumped from the bottom of the mines to these immense flat dams to evaporate in the sun and wind. Flamingos and seagulls travelled hundreds of miles from the ocean to settle on the salty shores of the dams and Victor and I could be on our own there.

'All I'm saying is that we're staying on in this bone-headed country but isn't it nice that there actually is a place called Malaga and why the hell shouldn't we think about it from time to time.'

'Better not to rush into anything.'

'Whatever you say.'

'So far it's not too bad for us here. At least we're making out.'

'Yes, that's the main thing. Here's our picnic spot. Switch the heater on. It's a fine place for a picnic you must admit.'

Victor brought the basket from the boot, his breath made foam in the dark air, and we started with brandy on the rocks. The heater gave out a faintly sulphureous smell. We chewed the dill pickles with our brandy, it was a cheerful mixture. The car was perched on the crest of the dam wall and the hard black water stretched to the horizon beneath the moon. A combination of exhaustion and contentment made us drink one brandy after the other and we talked about anything that came into our heads. I spread our dinner out between us while

Victor opened the wine. It was a red wine, Chateau Libertas, I remember. Our favourite wine, we drank it with everything, even scrambled egg and puddings. A vulgar affectation, said Frankie, who invariably reminded me to produce a dry white as well when he and Geoff came to dinner.

The grease from the salami on Victor's mouth left a very light smear on my own, I could taste it.

Down at the water's edge we made a tight ball of the salami rind and the wrapping paper and the bits and pieces we hadn't eaten and jammed it between two spiky rocks. A fragile net of ice was already shimmering in an inlet among the reeds. It was difficult to locate sound in the great space around us but somewhere a bird was shuffling through jagged grass. Our teeth were banging together with cold but something held us to the spot where we had buried the remains of our dinner and we went on crouching there. While we were panting up the wall back to the car Victor was saying, 'You know, why shouldn't we get us that knife – what do you think?'

'I think it's a fine idea if you think so. But I think we should get it soon. Otherwise they'll kill us first, if your pessimism is anything to go by.'

It was far too cold to talk any more so we broke into various bird calls in between bursts of laughter till we reached the car.

In the beginning it was Hazel Xoma who put me in the picture. She said, 'If you don't remember, it shows you were too young then to know about such things.'

'Honest, I've never heard of her,' I said.

'Dolores was just the type to make headlines. Now take me, I'm not the headline type.'

'Rubbish, there's nothing wrong with your voice.'

She sang sombre little contralto songs, not quite the sort that stop a show, but I didn't mind what I said to her off the surface of my mind as long as she told me whatever she knew.

'Wasn't just Dolores's voice that got her in the headlines, oh no!'

'Okay, then, there was a man involved or a scandal or something.'

'They go together, make no mistake. What kind of a scandal is it without a man? Mind you, I'll always give a person his due, even another girl. Dolores can sing like magic when it suits her.'

'Victor Butele doesn't look the type to lose his wife to someone else. Who was the other guy, Belafonte or someone?'

'Nonsense, he was a white man. When the show closed here Dolores had made herself into a star. The whole wide world wanted her. She behaved like a lady for the meantime and even the government fell for it. They gave her a passport to go and sing in Dar es Salaam and that's where she met this man. A proper big bug in politics who was also visiting in Dar es Salaam, how's that for timing? He came from Belgium, in the photos he looked a real sex bomb I'm telling you. Dolores had taken to white lamé at that time. Wigs were just coming in but she had other ideas. She shaved her head to the skin, she looked sixteen. Well, one sex bomb always catches another.'

'She married him, just like that?'

'She took off for Brussels with him and the headlines happened. The government hit the roof but Dolores said *I* must care? Victor gave her a divorce and kept the child. She was signing contracts all over the place, in top spots I'm telling you, but she took time off to marry this Belgian. More headlines. She lives in Rome now, on account of the rain in Belgium.'

'So there was a child?'

'One was more than enough for Dolores.' Hazel caught hold of her Adam's apple and said, 'What's the word for that thing inside here?'

'I'm hopeless at biology. Tonsils? Uvula?'

'No, man, they're somewhere else. You know the thing we singers have nightmares about.'

'Larynx?'

'Right. Dolores wasn't going to have any more babies

buggering about with her larynx.'

Dick Stanford wandered up chewing a dead pipe. 'So far scene six is the best thing in the show,' he said.

'Ag, Dick. You only say that because I'm not in it,' Hazel said.

Dick gave us that small personal smile that seemed to suggest a great mind turning over thoughts in meticulous procession. He was one of those men whose appearance stays constant despite a change of clothes. His off duty uniform of hairy tweed jacket, floppy flannels and Viyella shirt might just as well have been yet another dark suit accustomed to boardrooms. Someone who had known him since childhood had told me, once, that his late marriage was the result not so much of the war as an agony of mind about his path in life. While trying to decide whether or not to become an Anglican monk, he had met persuasive Gilbert Langenfelder who had snapped him up as executive material. After this came Margaret, a house near the polo club, children, horses, directorships. At chosen moments, with certain people, he was known to hark back to the time when his life might have taken either of two courses. This made me warm towards him all the more. I simply can't resist the attraction of people haunted by divisions in their lives.

While he and Hazel chatted about the show I nodded and smiled at appropriate moments, but the fine point of my concentration was on Victor Butele, drinking coffee with some of the cast at the other end of the hall. We had met earlier in a group and had said a few words to one another. I knew straight away that we would become friends. All my close friendships start in a flash. I believe in flashes of this sort. I read everything instinctually, I am completely non-intellectual, which from time to time I regret. Even at twenty I couldn't make head nor tail of the present without referring to the past. I sometimes think that every step I take is either an exact duplication of a former one or is a slightly filtered version of the same thing.

If I stare at him rudely enough, for long enough, he is

14

bound to look this way. He can't possibly be as entranced with those bird-brained chorus girls as he pretends to be. He's just being polite, in an old-fashioned way. There you are – I've caught his eye. There is no expression in his eyes whatsoever. He's tall enough to look right over the heads of the chorus girls, and that's precisely what he's doing. Age? At a guess, thirty-four. (You can never tell with Natives; anyway they never know themselves, my mother was inclined to blurt out when interrogating a prospective servant.) If I'd done what the family expected of me and stayed at home in dingy old Natal I wouldn't even be in a place like this, let alone with people like Dick, Margaret, Hazel, the rest of them. I'm happy in this tatty hall with its soggy ceiling and lousy smell from the blocked lavatory on the floor below. The filthy coffee they serve between scenes is fit for the gods. And the show we're putting on is going to be every bit as good as the last one, the one the old-stagers recall in reverent whispers as though it were the musical version of the Immaculate Conception.

'Hello Victor old chap. You know Hazel, of course. Do you know Ray Starle?'

'Yes, we met just now,' I said.

'We all arrived downstairs together. Talking of stairs, Dick,' Hazel said, 'the landing on the first floor's a disgrace. Not a window pane left. By July we'll be freezing to death in this place.'

'Can't the fund-raising committee spare a few cents?' I said.

Dick smiled paternally at us from behind the bowl of his pipe. 'Do you want window panes on the stairs or a new drop for scene four?'

Hazel said, 'We want both.'

'My dear girl, you can't have everything.'

'Why not?'

Dick's low grunty laugh. 'Madame Tebaldi, you're impossible.'

Hazel said, 'Tebaldi's voice is different to mine,' and I

turned aside to Victor Butele.

'Are you going to give the show a mention on your programme?' I asked him.

'Obviously you aren't one of my listeners. I have already.'

'I can follow Zulu. Up to a point. But none of the other languages.'

'The general impression is that my programme is in Zulu.'

His eyelids were lowered so as to cover half his eyes. Deliberately chilly, to keep me at a distance.

'Then I must tune in more often, mustn't I?'

He shrugged his shoulders. Dick and Hazel were examining a length of hessian that fell in lumpy folds from the outstretched arm of Len Silver, the set designer.

'Over to you.'

'In other words, what do you care?'

'I wouldn't put it like that exactly.'

The blood was beating away inside my face, I simply couldn't get it under control.

I said, 'But you'd like to.'

'When I want to be rude I'm much ruder than that.'

'You seem to be quite proud of the fact.'

Without the least warning, he was grinning at me. The last few minutes were suddenly wiped out, I felt dazed with relief. 'You and your ten million listeners,' I said.

'It isn't that, it's to do with you. It's just that you're a kid. An amateur.'

'What?'

His voice was now so low I could hardly hear him when he said, 'It doesn't matter that you're a kid, it fits the picture.'

I began to realise I was out of my depth, without in the least understanding why this should be so. In a panic I said, 'Would you like to come back to my place? I'll make tea or something.'

'Any reason why I should?'

I had no idea how to go on, so kept my mouth shut.

Victor looked down at his watch. Both his suit and tie were

an inky grey. The cuffs of his white shirt made dazzling circles round his wrists, which were darker than his face. Yes, you are like Aron, I repeated to myself. There's an eagle's beak inside your nose, but it's still a tribal nose. Aron had Indian blood too. This is quite rare, isn't it? Africans and Indians don't fuck each other, as a rule. The Indian blood shows in the length of your face and your ears. Hardly any lobes at all.

Well, the sight of him gave me a hard-on all right. But it wasn't lust pure and simple, there was something else that drew me over. He was the shocking dream that's called the unmentionable. This dream had become my Pole Star. Out of reach entirely, yet here it stood made flesh. Part of that flesh is the splendid curve of his cock. I absolutely reject the word unattainable.

'Okay, for say half an hour, and I don't drink tea,' he said.

'I put my cigarettes somewhere,' and I looked aside.

My hand was shaking ever so slightly as I made a grab at my cigarettes. I dropped the pack, picked it up and shoved it in my inside pocket.

'Love to Margaret,' I called to Dick and said goodnight to some of the others.

Victor was now passing through the doorway at the back of the hall. By the time I caught up with him he was circling the first landing, ferociously peering down at his shoes. I would willingly have called off the whole thing, there wasn't a grain of self-confidence left in me.

'See what Hazel means about the windows,' I said.

'Hazel's a honeybunch,' he said.

The building in which the group had its rooms was at the end of Von Brandis Street, in an area of warehouses and second-hand car lots. We stood with our hands in our pockets in Von Brandis Street while a dark cold wind pushed down the street from the north. The hands of a nightwatchman made huge shadows on a garage door as he ran them in and out of the flames that jumped through the holes of a tin can between his legs.

'I better follow you,' Victor said.

'You have a car?'

'How else do you think I get around?'

'You've made your point.' I tried to laugh at myself.

'My flat's in Killarney,' I said.

'Will it still be there?'

'What?'

He was walking away so I said, 'I'll go down Eloff into Bree, up Claim into Louis Botha. Then left at the Wilds, you know where? The block's in Seventh Street.'

In my rear mirror I watched the lights of his old Vauxhall bouncing up and down behind my Morris Minor, my first car. The movies weren't out yet so the streets were empty, just rows of immobile cars waiting beside the kerb under the lights. Tactfully, so I imagined, I drove slowly up Claim Street hill until he came right up behind me and hooted once, irritatedly. Curving down the road to the Wilds he was almost on my bumper and I swore into the mirror at him and revved abruptly and drew away from him, watching with angry pleasure his clouded headlights blur into the far distance. The street tracked here and there among the blocks of flats in Killarney and I swung into the basement garage of my block and began swabbing the chilly sweat off my forehead. I jumped out and ran into the street, frightened that he might have driven past.

We met in the entrance next to a bank of striped plants. Mirrors walled the lobby which was carpeted in dusty pink haircord. My eyes swarmed with several reflections of Victor's face, all of them aloof.

'Which floor?' a voice asked.

'The eighth,' I told him.

Without a backward glance he moved off down the lobby to the service lift. I followed, feeling humiliated on his behalf, and pressed the button on one of the Whites Only lifts. We waited, about a half dozen yards apart, facing separate doors in silence.

18

The two lifts reached the eighth floor simultaneously.

'How was yours?' Victor asked.

'Tremendous.'

'Mine too.'

He looked ahead down the open corridor and I dug in my pocket for my key. Inside my flat I turned to face him in the slip of a hall. 'What made you say "Will it still be there?" '

He laughed. 'What a fantastic memory you have.'

'You said it only twenty minutes ago and afterwards it struck me what a peculiar thing to say.'

He was leaning against the wall next to a print of Marchand's 'Quinces' and I noticed the limey yellow of the fruit picked out in the skin at the sides of his eyes. This amounted to nothing more than the cast of the light at that moment, however, for when he shifted his head the colour disappeared.

'The wind reminded me. When we were kids we lived in Sophiatown in a proper old shanty. On a windy day when we left for school one of us would be sure to crack the same old joke: "Will it still be there when we get back?" '

I smiled at him, but did not say anything.

'And I can tell you it always was, unfortunately!'

'You've got a pretty good memory too,' I said.

'One doesn't forget family jokes.'

'Big family?'

'I wouldn't know any more, we've scattered.'

'Where to?'

'Haven't a clue. I've got a lousy memory.'

We both half laughed.

'This is the sitting room.' I bent down to switch on a lamp. 'What can I get you?'

'Nice place you have.'

'I was lucky to – ' The explanation had too many twists and turns to it. I went on to say, 'The best part is the view.'

I pulled the curtain cord and we stood by the window. It was as though we were in a play, not like real life at all. On the other side of the window a lilo and some fuchsias in pots filled up the narrow porch. Down below were the tops of trees crackling in the wind and beyond them the comfortably spaced lights of the endless suburbs. For the first time since I had lived in the flat it was simply a view of lights anywhere, nothing more. I wondered what it was that had been taken away from it, and why.

I turned back into the room. 'You must be dying of thirst.'

I heard him behind me pacing this way and that.

'Brandy, gin, beer, coffee? Do sit down.'

'Thanks. I can't stay long.'

'What will it be?'

'Is coffee easy?'

'Don't you feel like a drink? It's been coffee all night so far.'

'What are you going to have?'

'Beer, I think. But that doesn't mean you must. Gin? I've got tonics.'

'No, coffee'll be fine.'

'Really? You sure?'

'Yes, coffee.'

'Maybe I'll have coffee too.'

I rushed from the centre of the room into the kitchen which, as in most flats, was off the entrance hall. What's *wrong* with you? I reached mechanically for things in cupboards. You're just a lousy host, that's what's wrong with you. Put your guest at ease, roll out the patter, man. Can't just let him sit there. Not a sound came out of my throat, witty or otherwise.

'Sorry, no cream.'

I plonked down the tray on a hideous little imbuia table. The flat was a furnished one, there was nothing in it of either beauty or value. Victor sat impassively in a cane chair with his long knuckly hands in his lap. My bookcase was right next to him, but apparently he had not inspected the titles while my back was turned. Even the magazines on the sofa lay in the same careless positions in which I had left them on going off to the rehearsal. When young and rough one longs for the object of one's love to ferret about for clues that round one out.

'White?'

'Just a couple of drops.'

I passed him a cup, the milk jug still at the ready in my hand. 'Like that?'

'Great.'

'It looks a bit strong.'

'No. No sugar.' He smiled.

And I thinking, you should do that more often, it's spectacular. Also it lets through a little bit of yourself, which makes a nice change. The one or two moments in which we had made tiny sparks fly earlier in the evening might never have happened for all the carry-over they had left behind. I, too, was responsible for this. I would not even look him in the eye. I could not face up to the possibility of a rejection. Furthermore, with this man, I was scared to death of the unknown.

'Tea,' he continued, 'keeps me awake at night.'

'That's odd, I always thought coffee was the thing that – '

Yes, he said, he lived in Soweto, where else? Official label: a township. But in actual fact bigger than white Johannesburg. Three-quarters of a million inhabitants. 'In a pitched battle, taking only numbers into account, Soweto would trounce Johannesburg,' he grinned. No, you couldn't get a house of your own if you were single, as he was. He rented a room from friends.

'More coffee?'

He jumped up, pulling down the cuffs of his shirt with two barely perceptible gestures.

'There's masses,' I said, idiotically.

'It's a long drive back. I'm up at five to get to work on time. And you?'

'About … seven.'

I watched the full length of his hipless back moving away towards the door. He doesn't know you need to be saved; to be frank, he has other things on his mind. I thought of dashing

21

after him, but strolled across the room nonchalantly instead. His fingers were fiddling with the doorknob.

'Thanks for coffee,' he said.

I blurted out, 'Are you free for lunch sometimes?'

'Never can tell in my sort of job what's going to turn up next.'

'Let's phone each other. I'll phone you.'

He shook his head and our eyes met for an instant. 'No, don't do that. Leave it to me. I'll phone you one of these days.'

'Will you?'

My office looked down on to a droopy fountain like a weak orgasm in a square of blackish green lawn in the well of the building. All around were the flanks of other buildings, several of them newer and slimmer than ours, but not one of them half as distinguished, so it was thought. In fact all the other mining corporations were regarded as rather common. The Jewishness of our tempestuous founding fathers had long since been watered down by Anglicanism, which was far smarter. Politically the tone was 'liberal', socially it was country clubbish (which ruled out Jews and Afrikaners anyhow). Salaries were lower than at opposition mining houses, the understanding being that prestige more than generously made up the difference.

April sunshine flooding in through two windows made my office a pleasant place in which to spend the lunch hour. Quite irrationally, I suppose, I believed that Victor Butele would take it as a good excuse for leaving no message if I happened to be out when he called, so I stayed put waiting for the phone to ring. I persuaded myself I'd heartlessly neglected college friends in Natal, not to mention my parents, so I bashed out wildly improbable accounts of the whirl of a life one was expected to lead in Johannesburg, posting them straight off without daring to read them back to myself. Life in Natal was both a million years ago and bang in the centre of every thought turning over in my head.

One of my mother's fixations is chiffon. She is wearing it the night I creep side by side with our new houseboy into the slit of an alley next to the coal shed. A certain slimy vine that I have never come across anywhere else trails over the roof of the shed. Moonlight comes and goes on the leaves of the vine and I start shivering with cold and excitement. My own pants are already round my feet, I feel foolish standing there with my tiny erection while the houseboy battles to untie the string round his waist.

Perhaps he isn't so interested in our adventure after all. If so, I can't understand the change in mood. For weeks and weeks we have been tracking one another through the garden. What we are doing now is the completely spontaneous development of what has gone before, or so it seems to me. At last he is free of his pants and he catches hold of my hand without another moment's hesitation. He takes control of my hand, leading it through the darkness. The breathtaking weight now in my hand strikes me not so much by its size, which is incomprehensible in my terms, as its silkiness. Naturally enough, I am deeply mortified by my own miserable pinhead of a thing (it has seemed perfectly acceptable up till now) and this takes away a great deal of the feeling of contentment that has come over me. Not a word is said between us and we simply stand there holding each other for a minute or two while laughter from my mother's dinner party reaches us as though from another planet.

As we walk into the blazing light of the kitchen my mother appears at the top of the steps and snaps, 'I told you to go to bed hours ago.'

She swoops over me to whisper, 'I wish you wouldn't spend so much time with the servants, it can't do you any good.'

What *does* she mean?

Her mind isn't really on me at all though, she has four courses to think about.

I slip into the space next to the fridge and watch her flipping up and banging down lids and peering into bowls. The cook and the other servants also watch her, they are afraid of her quick temper which people outside our own home know nothing about.

'Spoon,' she says.

The new houseboy is there first. He gives her a wooden spoon. The sight of his hand curved, now, round a mere spoon fascinates me. My mother takes the spoon without looking up. The impression I can't get rid of is of hands everywhere. Gradually my heartbeats slow down.

'Sauce good,' my mother says.

Her long white dress flows here and there as she strides round the silent room. I regard her as a great beauty, which she isn't really, though everyone admires her side view.

She says to the cook, 'All right. Five minutes.'

When she looks at me she is smiling because she has made up her mind, now, the meal will be a success. 'Darling, you look flushed. You're not getting another cold, are you?'

The houseboy towers behind her, I stare confusedly into two pairs of eyes. So what happens next, when suddenly there are two people whom you love?

'I must get back to them. You know how Daddy hates me to ...' She sails up the steps, her red fingernails picking at her skirt.

In Johannesburg I finished a letter to her, then immediately stretched out for the telephone and dialled the SABC. Barely a second between the two actions. Quite deliberately, I gave myself no time to change my mind.

A sulky Afrikaans voice said, 'To who?'

'Mr Butele. Victor Butele,' I repeated.

'Going through.'

The silence went on and on. Little scratches of sound made me half open my mouth to speak. If I waited long enough, he might come back from wherever he was and casually lift the

24

receiver and I would take him by surprise and trap him into agreeing to see me. But by phoning him I was disobeying him and the implications of this mistake began to dawn on me as the minutes passed by. Perhaps the fact that he was out meant that luck was on our side after all.

This conviction stayed with me throughout Easter, which came late that year. Somehow I knew it would be the last of the old Easters, from now on Easter would always be different. Spring is the season in which they say you can reasonably expect your life to begin again on some new axis, yet this happened to be autumn and here I was absolutely bursting with hope.

I visited friends, as though for the last time. I kept my secret to myself. Pink and white cosmos ran riot alongside the highways. Altogether there was a sort of candyfloss feeling in the air.

I filled in time at the rehearsal rooms. Often Len Silver was the only person there. He tacked dyed hessian to a frame and stood back to examine it through narrowed eyes. By throwing light at unheard of angles on to coarse fabric he made solids appear insubstantial. Partly he lived for his work in the theatre. He rationed his energy meticulously, the rest of it being used up by a political party, a tiny fragment of a party on which the authorities kept a watchful eye.

One early evening I couldn't bring myself to go back to my empty flat, which had become a purposeless place, and he was saying, 'They've got away at last, both of them.'

He mentioned two names, I had read about them in the newspaper once. I helped him carry the frame on to the stage. The hessian went up my nose in little flakes, it smelled of copper sulphate.

'Stuff this country, what do you say?' He snatched a tack from between his lips and plunged it into the frame.

He stepped to one side without taking his eyes off the drape. Transfer him to some other setting and he could have passed himself off as a rugby player. The one who plays hooker, sawn-off and chunky, but not heavy.

He said, 'I went to the Swazi border with them. We found a new route. No road signs and no moon but we found it.' He winked at me. 'It's in my head now!'

'Over there,' he said, 'the hammer.'

I passed him the hammer, he raised it above his head in such a way that one thought, when does the sacrifice begin? Footsteps scratched on the stairs. Victor's? I didn't turn my head, in the belief that self-discipline brings its own rewards. But it was one of the chorus arriving early. He flew through to the washroom.

Len Silver said, 'What's a good route this week might be a disaster next week. We have to keep ahead of the game!'

He went on in the same vein, it was for him both an exercise in keeping trim for the next job and uncoiling from the last one. My mind wandered, I have no sense of public responsibility.

'Between Ermelo and the border, that's the tricky bit.' I half heard him, whereas I should have paid attention. A long time later this all came back to me.

One day Dick's secretary came through on the office line. 'Mr Stanford for you, Ray.'

With my left hand I pasted a galley proof on to a layout sheet.

'Hello, Ray, can you spare a minute or two? Come right down, will you?'

On the executive floor of our building it was like sinking far far down into an ocean bed. Everything was sea green and hushed and faintly wavy. It was the carpeting that gave one the impression one was swaying powerlessly from side to side. As you swayed, your eyes tried to fasten on the faraway gleam of branches of light on the walls. A hefty bowl of oysterish flowers filled an alcove outside Dick's suite. His sparkling secretary switched off her typewriter and led me next door into his room.

No longer the bottom of the ocean but the earth's crust and its treasures. A surface of maize and gold with swirls of copper. On a straw-coloured wall an awesome map of South Africa picked out the Organisation's mines in wedges of polished wood. Dick's pipe blazed away between his teeth, the yellow smoke sloping obediently in the direction of an air-conditioning unit concealed somewhere.

'Victor, I think you know our future public relations director.'

Dick's capacity for acting both sly and blunt at the same time was a side of him I liked seeing in play. Nevertheless he could bring the blood into my face quicker than anyone else, Frankie included. One could hit back at Frankie and grab a laugh by doing so, but one was at a loss with Dick who directed an empire after all.

Victor Butele sat impassively with the balls of his fingers on Dick's desk.

'I'm serious, we think Ray may be quite useful one day. As long as he doesn't rush at things.'

Eventually Victor smiled across at me. He wore the same iron grey suit and white shirt with fat cuffs. I took the chair at the other end of the desk.

'Victor has a problem and I don't see why you shouldn't be the person to help him sort it out. Cigarette?'

The lid of the copper cigarette box was studded with a miniature gold bar set in a chip of basal reef, like a wart, and soon more smoke crowded the room.

'It isn't only his problem. It belongs to all of us. I'm grateful he's brought it up now and not left it till the last minute when it might have put us all into a bit of a spot. It's a question of seats at the opening night.'

'They're going fast,' I said.

'Almost too fast. Is the subcommittee doing anything about the families and friends of the cast? And what about the Africans who can afford opening night prices and would like to be there if only they could get their hands on some tickets?'

Victor said, 'People are complaining that the northern sub-urbs are turning the opening night into just another premiere for whites only.'

'This is unfortunate,' Dick said, 'and I won't have it.'

Naturally, he went on, we were looking for revenue. The group needed all the funds it could lay its hands on to carry on with the work it was doing. We must never lose sight of the group's original aim: to keep indigenous music and drama alive. Box office success depended very largely on white support. But how calamitous if we alienated the Africans, the very people for whose benefit the group was founded. And another point to be borne in mind. Did we not recognise the hostility in certain quarters – that 'official' public opinion which mistrusted our intentions, which considered us dangerous integrationists? How they would jump at any opportunity of exposing the slightest sign of dishonesty …

'I'll have a word with the chairman of the subcommittee this evening. And then, Ray, I want you to liaise with him about the details. See that at least a hundred seats are kept available. Not a block, spread them throughout the theatre. I can leave it to you?'

There was no doubt about it, I was flattered to be selected for the job, which is typical of me, or was.

The three of us were grouped at the door where a scarlet camellia floated in a copper dish and Dick said, 'What we want is an opening night with a family atmosphere.'

Victor and I went down the soundless passage past the beautiful ankles of the receptionist and came to the lifts.

Victor said, 'He's a solid rock to lean on.'

'We'd all be sunk without Dick. I wonder does he know this.'

We faced the lift but neither of us pressed the button. 'You didn't phone me, you promised you would,' I told him.

'I know.'

'Then why?'

I kept all this toneless. I witnessed myself in action. Me

at work. It takes the bloom off things when you can see this. But when there are no limits to the lengths you will go this is perhaps an advantage.

He said, 'I couldn't decide.'

'What?' I said.

'Shall we go outside somewhere?'

'We can go up to my office if you like.'

He shook his head and we wandered away to the stairs and down to the gloomy pillared hall that always reminded me of a biblical movie set past its best and out through the fussy bronze doors to the street. We set off between the high straight buildings of the financial district. A few people were straying about and the sun sloped down to the opposite pavement, leaving our side of the street in shade. This district of the city ends abruptly and all of a sudden you are in a shambly open space blocked off by the cinnamon-coloured dumps of dead mines.

'Have you ever been into this crazy church behind the parking lot? Hardly anyone knows it's even there. Dick knows about it. Someone said she sees him popping in there for a few minutes on his way home. It's high Anglican, like him. It must have been one of the smart churches in the gold rush days.'

'Are you Anglican?' he asked.

'No, Catholic. I mean I'm nothing really. I went to a Catholic boarding school but long before I'd even left there I'd decided to give it up and I did. And you?'

'Nothing.'

'But before you were nothing?'

'Nothing again.'

'But you must have been something. Everyone is.'

'My father used to mutter something about the guiding light of the psalms but no one paid him much attention.'

A red dusty track passed between railings into a square of sand and there was the church. Opposite stood a tiny elegant mine headgear of about 1900.

Victor said, 'Is it all right to go inside?'

'I can't think of anywhere else at the moment.'

Veins of dirt ran this way and that all over the porch and we stepped over the wildly tilting flagstones into the aisle and sat down in the back pew. Next to us was a strange black cupboard which might have been a confessional. Once we had settled down the creaking stopped and there wasn't a sound in the church. An air of impermanence came across very strongly. For some time we stared around us almost reverently, as one can't help doing in churches, no matter how removed you might be from what they stand for.

'I really thought you would phone me,' I said. 'I couldn't understand it when nothing happened.'

'I nearly did the next day. Then I put it off. I needed time to work it all out.'

'What were you working out?'

'Plenty of things. It takes time, you know.'

'But you did want us to meet again, didn't you?'

'Why do you think I came to see Dick today?'

'To fix up about those seats, I suppose.'

'I knew he'd bring you into the picture sooner or later. I put off phoning you for so long I thought I'd better do it some other way.' For the first time since I had known him he laughed without any strain or affectation whatsoever. 'You see how I can complicate things when I try!'

'Well, it does seem a rather roundabout way of – '

'For all I knew, you were just another hot white boy who liked black cocks.'

'Are there lots of them like that?'

'Nobody's actually done a survey.'

'Take you, for example. Do they make passes at you regularly?'

'It happens. Not every day.'

'And tell me ...' I was absolutely floored, but anxious not to show it, '... what do you do about it? I mean, how many have you actually had?'

'Two,' he said, promptly.

'I must say, you are frank.'

'We're being honest with each other, aren't we? If we're not, what's the point of all this?'

The pace he had set made my brain work slowly, instead of the reverse, which was what was required.

'They wanted to be fucked and I fucked them. Is that all it amounts to with you too?'

'No,' I said, 'no it isn't.'

'You sure?'

'Yes, I am.'

'You reckon I'm worth more than just bed?'

'Yes, I do. At least I hope you are. But bed comes into it too. What do you think about it?'

'Much the same as you.'

'Good.'

'That's all I wanted to know. To start with.'

'What would you have done if I'd said yes? To your first question.'

He looked me up and down with an ironic expression playing round his mouth. 'You're a handsome boy. Anyone can get a hard-on. Maybe we could have done it together. Once or twice. So what?'

'You've been married,' I said. 'You've got a child, Hazel told me.'

'What's that got to do with it?'

'I don't know, I've never asked anyone before.'

'We can talk about that later, there's lots of time.'

The sense of calm that came from him made me terribly happy. I had no means of telling how much this cost him. I put my hand over his, which was as still as a stone.

We went outside and crossed through the waste ground and walked up the street where noonday traffic was suddenly screeching in both directions. Our building appeared round the corner far too quickly. Facing a parting with him was different now.

'Don't you forget about those seats,' he said.

We both loved Dick, but we couldn't help laughing at the trick Victor had played on him. There seemed no limits, then, to our partnership against the world.

When I turned aside a woman in a floral printed dress was glancing over us, then she went on her way.

'You and I have employers and jobs to do,' Victor said.

'Hell, if only we hadn't.'

We signalled to each other so surreptitiously that the movement of each eyelid must surely have been invisible to everyone but ourselves.

After that we were always together though, needless to say, we couldn't meet in any place that struck our fancy. To be exact, there were only two places where we could meet, either at the group's rooms during rehearsals or afterwards at my flat. We were feeling our way not only with each other but around the crags and pits of daily living and, taking into account the obvious restrictions, it was astonishingly easy and untroubled and we simply coasted along in between our meetings. Victor often laughed aloud in the dark. In our vacuum we lived off layer upon layer of strength that did not seem to have been there before.

I had been poised expectantly in one direction for so long that, when we made love, what was happening, at any rate for me, was a bridging of the division between thought and action.

Victor did not resist any more. He was no longer wary. He turned aside from preoccupations that had preceded me without a backward glance, it seemed. The very thought of his life got him down, he told me once. Same town, same job, same people. Was I a turning point? He smiled when he said this. He wanted to lose sight of everything outside the room in which we were lying half asleep. I tried to as well. So much of our energy was taken up in this way. But we didn't mind. We told each other this often. And so there it was, he fell in with me.

May arrived, the leaves roared down out of the trees. Sundays were the best days. We stayed put in the flat. The early winter days seemed lovelier than ever and my porch was entirely shut off from the rest of the block and we lay about in the sun for hours on end, drinking iced beer and splitting the various sections of the newspapers between us. Though we bought every paper and never missed a word in any of them, the events they reported seemed to be happening to strangers with whom we could not possibly concern ourselves. After I had cooked eggs on Sunday night Victor left the building in the service lift and walked round the corner to the side street where he parked his car.

Voices gave the clue, Victor said. You could pin down a person by his voice. As a township schoolboy he had paid attention to the voices on the radio. The radio announcers were ex-schoolteachers in those days. They enunciated carefully, they did nothing at all with their voices. Listeners everywhere looked blankly at their radio sets. He went from school to Broadcast House as a messenger. Without a bike at first. Then he rose a step, they gave him a bike. When his voice deepened he could make it growl confidentially. He forced himself past the ex-schoolteachers to someone who would listen to him. And so he became the first announcer who did not enunciate with care. Beside me in the room he mocked himself.

'A voiceless man with a carrying voice.' He stopped speaking to smile again, I passed the tips of my fingers across his teeth.

In a panic that he might disbelieve his hold over me, my head darted down to draw his cock into my mouth. I learnt about Victor through his body. All the bodies before him had led no further, I had not even reached the stage of feeling at home with them. By growing to know Victor's body I came to trust him. When I first met Victor I was not only edgy in bed but inefficient. He had said, 'I know your type, the emotional type. Too much emotion, man. Cut down the emotion. You'll feel better about it if you do.' I followed his lead, and he got me over this stage, to another, a completely new area that I had not been aware of.

The curtains crept stealthily forwards and backwards in a breeze. My feeling for him became more clearly defined the more time we spent together. I would stand guard over him. I would not let bullies get anywhere near him.

I went to Broadcast House to see where Victor worked. The administrators were either genuinely proud of their tyranny or secretly troubled by it, I could never quite make this out. At any rate they encouraged visitors to inspect the place for themselves. From afar the building had always looked no grimmer than a moderately enlightened prison but when you came closer all it resembled was a dumpy woman in grey felt who should have gone on a diet long ago. Several of the women were the dead spit of the building itself, though we were permitted to come face to face only with those who happened to be passing through the public rooms at that moment. Victor's territory was restricted to Radio Bantu which was cordoned off in another part of the building with its separate entrance in a less imposing street.

Victor's closest friend among his colleagues was Theo Futa, a fat fluttery man with ten children. When I met him that day I was convinced that marriage and all those children represented a desperate womanish flight from his real inclinations. But Victor assured me I was wrong, that Theo's squeaks and sighs amounted to nothing more than a mannerism that had sneaked up on him unawares.

'Victor tells me you feed him plenty material from the show,' he said.

'Do you think it's worth using?' I asked.

'From the cuts – well, it sounds like a nice show.'

'It better be, or else.'

Theo shook all over. 'How do you like this place?'

'It's like Grand Central Station.'

'So you been in New York?'

'Not really.'

Theo giggled. 'Just a manner of speaking, hey.' He blinked

at me with his creased up eyes.

He said, 'You have a quiet office, I bet.'

'It's like a morgue.'

'This is no time to speak of death. You have youth on your side!'

Next to me Victor was shifting his feet about, though not impatiently.

'How're your children?' I said.

'You want me to go through them one by one?' A phlegmy chuckle trembled in Theo's throat. 'Hey, you're a real tonic. That's what Victor says.'

'Does he?'

'Victor's a different guy since he got tied up with your show. Just look at him. He's a kid again.'

Victor whistled very softly. 'Ray didn't come here to listen to rubbish. This is an instructional tour.'

But Theo was still beaming at me. He seemed entirely released, as though revelling in the sensation of being wide open to whatever was blown across his path, and all of a sudden I had placed him on a pedestal because Victor's welfare was something he cared about.

'See you,' I said, and immediately wished I had put it more formally.

Passages that were neither dirty nor clean led on and on to similar passages. Victor shared a room with two other announcers who broadcast in Sotho and Xhosa. No one else was there at the time and I stood next to Victor's desk looking down at his fan mail. Neat wodges of postcards held together by rubber bands surrounded his typewriter. The writing on all the postcards had the same forlorn quality, or was this simply the patronising side of my imagination insisting on making it so? I noticed that Victor's postcards far outnumbered those on the other desks and I felt proud of his popularity without pausing to consider the irrelevance of this emotion.

We went in and out of rooms, some of which were called studios, though they all looked extraordinarily alike. All one could assume was that the bleak uniformity was there for a purpose. Occasionally I was told to peer through glass at announcers making gestures in front of microphones. Even without hearing a word of what they were saying you knew it was either drivel or lies, trimmed into this state by some governor or other, and behind him by a ministry in Pretoria. It was all so dead and alive I could hardly wait to get out of the place.

Then I told myself, look at it from his point of view, he earns his living here.

I said, 'What can one say except that it's in a class of its own?' and we stepped into the street where I took in a great wave of fresh air that made me feel giddy one minute, then brought on a craving for sex in the next.

I felt I did not know anything about myself. I was convinced of one thing only that, no matter what, I would come to no good in the end.

Near a block of warehouses Africans were streaming into a doorway. Flies drifted this way and that on the other side of a window scrawled with lettering. There is a special grimy smell that hits you long before you reach one of these corner eating houses. They are always on corners, in every town. Hotela lo Bantu. Bantu restaurant. Offal and onions and shit-coloured walls. Nervy white stomachs reel away from the blast groping for breath. Victor and I passed the main entrance and he steered me through a slit in the wall into darkness. We stood there for a few seconds. I saw Victor's beautiful hands parting a curtain of seashells threaded through string and a man with greased sideburns appeared out of nowhere and flashed his teeth at us.

'Hail one and all!'

His skin, too, looked greased. A black boot polish face. I distrusted him straightaway.

'Ray Starle, PRO; Siegfried Ngoya, restaurateur.'

I made him shake hands, I was afraid in case Victor should know how I felt about this man.

I fingered the curtain admiringly to gain time.

'And so, old Vic, how's the Voice of America?'

We went through into a boxy room with half a dozen tables. Some men in chalk-stripe suits crouched over their food in a corner. One of them carried on talking while the others listened.

I said to Victor, 'Is it all right for me to be here – it won't land someone in court or worse?'

Siegfried Ngoya wheeled round chanting with laughter. 'Man, this isn't the Dark Ages!'

I said, 'It's hard to tell sometimes.'

'If you keep your chin up you can still get by.'

'By how much?'

'Look at me!'

Siegfried Ngoya's teeth seemed to fill the whole room, let alone his face. 'Vic's guests are my friends and vice versa. Make yourself at home.'

After my first beer I began to enjoy myself and Siegfried joined another table, still shouting his head off.

Victor said, 'He's on to a good thing here. He's made a packet. The white liberals get a kick out of it and they bring overseas journalists here in droves and it's at least somewhere for us to have a steak. The steak's good, you wait.'

'I bet you eat a lot of rubbish the rest of the time.'

'Whoever invented toasted sandwiches should be made a Sir. Otherwise have his balls cut off and put in the sandwiches.'

'I knew this person who owned a snack bar. He made four hundred per cent profit on toasted sandwiches. They put all the crap they can get hold of into toasted sandwiches.'

'Haven't killed me off yet.'

'On Monday mornings at this snack bar they used to sponge down Saturday's cakes and serve them up as fresh.'

'That's a dirty trick. How's your beer?'

I put my hand over the top of my glass. My other hand was safely out of sight under the table gripping my kneecap.

'Victor?'

'Ja.'

'Listen.'

'Am I talking too much?'

'I've got a great idea. This way we can cut toasted sandwiches out of your life and clear up your transport problem in one fell swoop. What I've – '

'I'm used to getting up early. As for – '

'Yes, you are talking too much. What I was trying to say is, why don't we sort of team up. I mean, what about us getting a house or something. What I feel is, if you don't try, if you don't try to carry things off then you might as well give up altogether, there just isn't any point to anything.'

Victor said, 'How's that hole in your head coming along?'

'Please,' I said, 'don't interrupt the whole time.'

'I wasn't. You'd stopped, and so I thought I'd better say something.'

'I hadn't stopped,' I said.

Victor shrugged his shoulders while he glanced up at the ceiling. He drank the rest of his beer.

I said, 'Aren't you interested in my idea?'

A waiter in a khaki apron made a sign with his forefinger and Victor said to me, 'Go on. Our steaks will be here any minute now.'

'I can fix it,' I said. I was filled with that madcap sense of power that accompanies the early days of love when you are Hannibal and the Alps are molehills. By loving Victor I meant, I suppose, that I saw myself as responsible for his happiness. I said, 'I've thought about it from every angle under the sun and nothing's impossible and there must be a house somewhere – well, I just know there is.'

Victor slipped his chin into the outstretched palms of his hands, which was an unfamiliar gesture for him, and looked me over with a rather superior air. 'You know what I know? I know you could marry a beautiful rich girl and live in a beautiful big house that you wouldn't have to pay for. Her dad would pay.'

'Now it's your turn. Go on.'

'Yes, if you can't bring it off with the Langenfelder girl take your pick down the line. Man, this town's full of rich girls on the lookout for a handsome boy with a bright future.'

'Must be my unlucky day. The Langenfelder girl got engaged this morning.'

'So? What's wrong with you? Break it up, man.'

'I couldn't do that. They say they're mad about each other. And you know me, I'm a sucker for things like that.'

'Any psychiatrist can cure you on the turn.'

Victor dropped his hands to the table with a faint clap. The mocking look in his eyes was no longer there, he seemed exhausted and sad all of a sudden and I was afraid that I might lose hold of the situation if it were played on some other level, played straight in fact. He said, 'To hell with the Langenfelder girl and the rest of that bunch. Look around. Find a girl who's your type. Settle down. Have a couple of kids. Marriage isn't so bad. Do it, Ray.'

'No.'

'I'm telling you what's for the best.'

'I think it's very kind of you to worry so much. What you're saying sounds very sensible. But I'm not going to do it.'

'You're crazy if you don't join in and do what everybody else does.'

'Not everybody.'

All he wanted to do was to put me on the right tack, for my own sake, Victor said.

I'd never been loved in the way I believed one should be loved. With my parents, it had always been a matter of my growing up exactly like themselves in every way, they could see no reason why I shouldn't, and it was this image that they cared about and presumably loved. There was nothing remotely like this with Victor and the absence of it gave me enormous confidence in myself as well as in my capacity to provide him with whatever it was he required.

I thanked him, but I had made up my mind, I told him.

'Aren't you excited?' I asked him. 'Aren't you even looking forward to it a bit?'

He smiled, though you could still see the tiredness in his face.

He said, 'I don't stand a chance with you, do I?'

'Say that again.'

'Since when have you been deaf? Anyway, Frankie, there isn't time.'

Frankie did not know about the woman in the lift who had said to me yesterday, 'We haven't met. I'm in 816.'

I glanced sideways at her ancient bright cockatoo face, then down at her poodle.

'Are you? I'm on the same floor.'

'Yes, I know you by sight. My flat's at the end. The corner one. I've always had a corner flat. I was in Manhattan Court before here.'

The lift doors opened at the eighth floor, we set off down the corridor.

Then she started. 'A Native has been in your flat. Twice,' she said.

Native. Not so much the word itself as the way it whisked off her tongue. All their tongues get shot of the word in this way, so you'd think one would be used to it by now. Cat. Hat. Spade. Native.

'The cleaner?' I said.

'Oh no. Cherie knows the cleaner. It wasn't the cleaner. Cherie barked at him. He was quite a well-dressed Native.'

'He certainly is! Simon. From our office. Non-European personnel section. He's clothes mad.'

'Very sure of himself. I know that type.'

'He came to deliver some files, if I remember.'

'Natives wandering round a block of flats create a bad impression.' We slowed down at my front door. 'A year ago this block was crawling with them. Always coming and going and cheeky too. People on the fifth floor were Communists.

40

Running a Communist cell right here in this building. Thank goodness the police aren't so asleep as people think.'

I kept my eyes on my key which was twirling wildly round my finger. 'How old is Cherie?' I said. She's the brains in the family. And a hundred years younger than you, you evil old cunt. 'I could just eat her.'

'Everybody loves Cherie. Bye now.'

Cherie's cerise bow matched her anus and I closed my eyes to the sight and went inside my flat, seething, and closed the door very softly.

'Oh,' cried Frankie, 'no time for your old aunt any more. The aunt who scooped you on to her broomstick the very minute you hit this town because she knew you were far too special to go down into the mud with the rest of them.'

'I'm sorry, I put it badly,' I said.

'I must say I've known you to put things better.'

I jumped up and stood in a gap between damask curtains and thought how ordered Frankie's life was and for a split second I envied him. The house was Geoff's but registered in Frankie's name. Ours, he said, is a proper marriage. How many times have I said to Merle, Merle, you can't do better than marry a medic? What *they* don't know about biology. But sure, I'm a business girl too. If you don't produce enfants within the first three years you've just got to grit your teeth and grin and bear it and go into business. But I never never never bring business into my home. Won't those movie stars ever *learn*? Even the Oliviers. I could've *died* for Vivien.

'You're just a bundle of nerves, petal.'

The smoky afternoon light came off the tops of the trees. Or was it sifting down to meet the trees? Far away beyond the last suburbs were the feathery mountains and surely between here and there was a house that was just right for us.

Frankie tickled the back of my neck. Whenever I catch a whiff of Jolie Madame I remember Frankie. 'So you've gone and given up that cosy rent-controlled flat we found you. And you've gone and broken up some perfectly respectable marriage and now you're in a twit because you're not sure whether or not he's going to make it legal, right?'

I said, 'He was divorced years ago and all we want is a shut off house in a quiet street with a bit of garden and some trees.'

'Easy. Give him the measurements and tell him to go out and get it.'

'I said I'd find it. It's easier for me.'

'Buy, presumably.'

'No, to rent.'

'But owning a house is so much more solid. Who is this guy anyway?'

'He's in radio. He has whole programmes all to himself.'

'Some sort of disc jockey?' Frankie's triangular black eyes looked me up and down rather hectically. 'Sweetheart, I've always wanted the best for you and you're pretty enough and nice enough to get it. As they used to say to Barbara Stanwyck, you're not making some awful mistake, are you?'

'In any case I love him,' I said.

'No need to get so touchy. Tell me more about him.'

'He's black.'

'Where?'

I felt myself going very cold and hard, I tried to resist this.

'Well, he's black, what more do you want to know?'

'Sorry, sugar, while I find my ear trumpet. Let's start from the beginning again.'

'Black. Isn't that one of the ways of describing an African?'

'Liebe Gott.'

Frankie stuffed half his fist into his mouth, then he took it out again, it was spotted with bite-marks.

Several seconds passed while he stared at me.

'So what they say about a nigra's size is true, is it?'

'Thanks for the tea,' I said.

'You and a buck nigger. *Marriage?*'

I couldn't take it after that and ran outside to my car and drove away. I drove anywhere for a while. Traffic lights and trees and front gates and Frankie's screams and more and more stop signs. He'll get over it and you've just got to remember to be practical about these things, the effect on certain people whose lives cruise along steady courses, and I don't blame him one bit. The shock. That's all. I wish Victor were here. I can't live without him and I've lost my balance in the rush. I'll get it back any minute now.

When I spotted a telephone booth I drew up and went inside and called an estate agent. I had paper and pen ready and I wrote down the addresses of the houses he read out to me. All the houses were in the northern suburbs because something told me we would be safest there. I specifically asked for suburbs that were ever so slightly running to seed. Rents were lower and I associated them with undergrowth and high thick hedges and these were the suburbs where the only liberal people I knew of seemed to live. Going over this now, it seems a muddled line of thought but nothing made sense whichever way you looked at it, and I can't imagine what other line one could have taken. Everything was ranked dead against us, and this was the last thing I wanted to admit.

The fourth house was the right one. A wall that needed a coat of paint hid it from the street and parts of another wall and a shaggy cypress hedge bordered the rest of the property. 'We're off to Minorca,' the woman said, 'for a year.' I thought she must have pronounced it wrongly and asked her to repeat it. 'I know, everyone imagines we mean Majorca. But Majorca's phony now and in any case we couldn't afford it there. My husband's a painter. He teaches at art school. He has to.' Rooms careered off in unexpected directions though it wasn't a large house. Our shoes sounded on stripped wooden floors, high above us I could make out leaves and grapes on moulded ceilings. From the kitchen door, there it was – a servant's khaya, absolutely essential to the plan by which we would have to run our lives. When I stood in the middle of the back lawn the privacy of it all brought my heart into my mouth. And there was a tennis court. Scabs of old moss dotted the service line. I turned to the woman, who was watching me strangely.

'I'll take five rands a month off the rent,' she said.

'But you mustn't, you'll need it in Minorca.'

'No, I'd like to, you look so happy.'

Inside the house the odour of decayed geraniums came in from the garden. 'For a time we thought no one would take the house. Isn't everyone's cup of tea.' She wore her hair in middle-aged pigtails and her eyes were the colour of freckles. 'You'll have to take it partly furnished,' she said. 'That'd suit us,' I told her. 'Don't tell me you're about to get married,' she laughed. I began to laugh too, I was feeling a bit light-headed. 'Just my cousin and me. He's American,' I said. Luckily for me I not only love making up lies but get a certain pleasure out of lying triumphantly. It takes you out of yourself. 'There are lots of pitfalls. I'll start with the ants,' she said.

It was the most wonderful day of my life, I had enough energy to keep going for a week. Victor and I stood in the rather greying sitting room and hugged each other. The bewildered air with which he had trailed round the house and garden earlier in the day had left him.

'Pinch me,' he said. He looked about sixteen years old.

He held out his arm, which was most beautifully proportioned and shaded. He was wearing a T-shirt with tight elastic cuffs that left a very faint criss-cross pattern on the muscle of his upper arm.

I said, 'You've still got my tin trunk to carry.'

'Yes, boss.'

'I must make one last trip to the flat. You can have a beer ready when I get back.'

'You're doing all the work,' he said.

'Not for long.'

He followed me to the door. 'You've done everything,' he said.

'Talk shit,' I said.

He stayed inside the doorway and I felt a finger running reflectively down my spine to the small hump of bone at the base, one of my sensitive spots. 'Drive carefully, man.'

When I woke up in the morning in our house I knew exactly where I was. I am constantly being taken by surprise, but never by dreams that have been converted into reality. Illusion, still, or the real thing? I never ask myself that question. These two states flow in and out of my mind as a matter of course. You are very slightly round the bend all the time, I was once told by a pompous friend who was halfway through a psychology degree.

I climbed out of bed to make coffee. A Sunday, the first of the month. Even the days of the week had fallen appropriately for our move into the house. On the other side of the curtain sunshine was creeping up the lawn. A wardrobe, a strip of carpet that felt as worn as flannel under your feet, an indigo pottery lamp next to the bed. A vast floppy double bed. An acre of bed on which to leave our stains, to fly away on. Passing the mirror I caught a glimpse of Victor flat out on the bed. I stopped short, went back to the mirror. He was sound asleep and his reflection took him miles away from me. This glass must either be a very cheap one or designed to scare you like the wobbly one at the Victory Cavalcade. I turned away from it. Looked across at the man himself. My lover in our bed. Aron was not in *my* bed, the bed was the nanny's.

My sister is screaming in the middle of the night and I wake up and lie there listening to the senseless racket. We have left the town house for a sort of country seat well outside the town where we can have horses, which is smart. My sister's room is next to mine in the nursery wing. On the other side of her room is the nanny's room, the house ends there. 'Fay, the baby's crying,' I shout in the darkness. I try again, my voice is slapped right back at me. I jump out of bed and shiver, though it is a warm night. The door of Fay's room is shut and I yell, 'Fay.' I push open the door in exasperation and find the light switch and snap it on. The compact little cell is ablaze with light. Two stark naked brown bodies fill up the bed on top of a white sheet. Fay is mountainous and, being Cape Coloured, is the lighter of the two. Aron's balls and cock are strewn languidly between his long stuck apart legs and the next minute he is sitting up in bed and the whites of his eyes make me tremble, as eyes do in dreams. The shock of discovery, for both of us. My world has caved in. Now of course he will murder me, murder is second nature to them. I can think of nothing but flight. I hurtle up the passage, through several rooms, into another wing.

I love my home, I know the precise position of every stick of furniture. In the dark I sidestep with stunning dexterity.

'Dad, the baby's crying and one of the farm boys is in Fay's room.'

Oh you stupid tit, don't you know he's a lawyer? Lawyers miss nothing, certainly not statements on which an entire prosecution can be constructed. Just one word – if only I could take it back. 'One of the farm boys?' is already what he is repeating.

This particular farm boy has got away, naturally enough, and Fay in her Chinese rayon dressing gown is stroking the baby whom she is devoted to and whom she calls 'skatjie' and 'cock-a-doodle-doo' and I am put back to bed with fingers sliding to and fro across my forehead. 'What a horrid thing to happen to you, that beastly Fay. One never knows with these girls. And all that rubbish about being a Presbyterian. You can tell Daddy all about it in the morning, my darling.'

I don't want to tell him anything in the morning. I want things to go on as they were before.

A farm knocks a town child for a six. All those elemental goings-on, for instance. You toss off the discovery, only to brood about it later. And, of the farm gang, I am aware of Aron from the beginning. He picks up a scent from me too – we raise eyebrows at one another behind the others' backs. At school the hymns are in Latin, my eye wanders again and again to the translation in the next column. 'I am black but beautiful O daughter of Jerusalem therefore the king loved me and took me into his chamber.' I transpose sexes to suit myself but that is by the way, it is really the mystery behind the scene that matters most.

Aron is by far the tallest of the gang and it is the Indian blood in him that gives him those sloped eyes and satin side-burns. His clothes are as ragged as the others. They all live in a compound beyond the milking shed. My father is adamant that I should ride well. Aron understands horses. He is my groom. A saddle is chosen.

We ride through hot stinging grass. The farm is all hillsides and valleys; it is not good riding country but we have our orders. His presence overwhelms me – much more so than that of the horse, though they are of a type of course. I have never cantered before and I start doing so now. Red kaffirboom and wattle flower tear past me in the opposite direction and I can't take the anxiety another minute and willingly fall off the horse. I am a natural for falling off horses. I slide loosely through the grass and am on my feet again almost immediately. Aron reaches me with hands outstretched. I am motionless while he pats me all over, testing for broken bones presumably.

The flat of one of his hands is wide enough to cover the entire surface of my stomach. Through a tear in his overalls I notice the huge glimmering knuckle of his breastbone. His skin odour streams towards me, I am not repelled by it as other people are. They complain angrily when trapped by it. What worries me is that my father might blame Aron for my having fallen, whereas it had nothing to do with him. I take the present, a cigarette lighter, from my shirt pocket and give it to him and he slips it from one hand to the other with a smile round his mouth – nothing surprises him. How quiet it is down there in the grass and I am in love and wish Aron would make some devastating gesture or other from which neither of us would ever be able to retreat. He continues to throw little sideways smiles at me and I am held back by precedent and convention and sheer boneheadedness. We simply walk the horse home in the end.

'Now you just pop down to the compound with Daddy and give him all the help you can and breakfast will be ready when you get back. Scrambled or poached?'

My father is a self-made man who always appears to be in complete control of himself. He frequently laughs, but he never lets himself go. He extends this form of behaviour into a whole code of living. He married too young perhaps; worry and ambition grate together inside him. He is prematurely bald and smokes before breakfast. He marches me into the farmyard where the induna has lined up the gang next to the milking shed and I hate him.

Quite gently he says to me, 'Which one?'

A dozen expressionless faces. He could so easily have run off during the night, why hasn't he? Taking his punishment like a man, or making sure that I should? Or is it all just a joke to him?

Click click. Your stupid sour heart is the recorder now. It's wounded, or so you believe. He prefers Fay to you. You simply can't take this. Won't. You're a masochist as well and you love him right up till the end. I point to Aron and never see him again.

Afterwards I stay in my room. I throw up meal after meal, I hear the doctor say to my mother, 'All the symptoms of nervous collapse.'

'Rubbish,' she snorts, 'we aren't a family for that sort of thing.'

'My dear Stella. His temperament. He's excitable, we've always accepted that.'

'But nerves. At his age. He's still a brat. Heavens above, we're not talking about an adult. He's *twelve*.'

All the same she is very patient. She dashes in and out with soup and books. She gives me that hesitant attention that reveals she has no idea what it's all about and after a week or two she decides the only remedy is tennis. She sets out to turn me into a junior tennis champion. Having pulled this off she is delighted with both herself and with me.

I said to Victor, 'Coffee?'

I got back into bed, balancing the tray on my knees. I said, 'I've broken the sugar basin.'

'We can give up sugar,' he said.

'And make our friends do the same?'

'Who are our friends?'

'I don't know.'

Victor laughed. He slid under the blankets again and pushed his face into the side of my leg and then lay still, tucked up against me, as though he were thinking.

'Coffee's getting cold,' I said after a while.

'I'm happy,' he mumbled.

I thought about his being older than me and that, on account of this, he would be the first to die.

He sat up again and stretched himself and I gave him his coffee. His eyes were childlike in the mornings.

I said, 'There's one hell of a lot to get done today.'

'Yes, boss. I'm going to help you today.'

I was searching among the blankets for my cigarettes.

Victor said, 'Let's have a black and white house. How's that for a joke?'

'No one could say it isn't sick enough.'

'White walls and black furniture and white carpets and black frames round white pictures. All we need is a pot of paint.'

'You're a racist. You can't get race out of your head, can you?'

'Do you find this unexpected?' he said.

He held out his cup for more coffee. The sun reached the window sill, then darted between a slit in the curtains.

'Sorry,' I said, 'it was just a remark.'

'Don't back down. You're probably right.'

'That's impossible.'

'And yourself? How do you classify yourself?' he said.

'Listen,' I said, 'if either of us was bothered about race we wouldn't be here in this bed.'

'I'm not so sure. Maybe the fact that we are in this bed proves a point in itself.'

'What point?'

He smiled sourly. 'That you and I are racists,' he said.

'Talk shit,' I said.

At the opening night the leading lady novelist said, 'It's soft-centred, that's the disappointment.'

'It's what? I enjoyed it enormously.'

'Their first production was raw and untrimmed and it pumped good red blood. It was the real thing.'

'Whatever you say. But I much preferred this one. So full of life.'

'Surface vitality isn't life. That's half the trouble, it's too polished where it needn't be. As for the lyrics – third-rate Broadway, only more pretentious.'

Moonlight barely touched the Corinthian columns and in the crowd moving down the steps I could put a finger into Victor's half-closed hand for a second or two. On the other side of me Margaret was murmuring, 'I'm bowled over. The punch of it all bowls you over.'

She said, 'Hubert's music is ... what is it? Urban Africa with longings that are tied up with somewhere else we don't know about.'

Dick jutted round her shoulder to bring Victor into the swim. He always made a point of this. Not only with Victor but with all Africans. 'What do you think of it?'

We came to a stop on the steps, all around us people were terribly excited. 'It should do well,' I heard Victor say.

'It's more than just a folk musical. The music has storm clouds behind it,' Margaret was saying.

Dick said, 'Hazel was superb tonight. I've never heard her in better voice.'

We reached the driveway in front of the steps. The crowd was still rolling out of the hall behind us. About every fifth person was black; this must have pleased Dick. He had got the sort of opening night he had wanted and this showed in his happy craggy face. You couldn't really expect to keep out the sable stoles and emerald pendants altogether, but the Swazi homecraft shawls and lumps of pottery swinging on leather thongs down to the navel outnumbered them ten to one. Of course the university hall did have a very special sort of atmosphere, or so it was claimed. Somehow it always managed to attract a more *serious* audience than the theatres downtown. A certain freedom in the air: can't you feel it? The fact that one was permitted to have an audience that was *mixed* ... well, it wasn't like being in South Africa at all. Makes one feel rather good inside, you know, relaxed ...

Dick said, 'The cast are joining us as soon as they've taken off their warpaint.'

The show had led Margaret into other worlds, even though only for the time being. She was tramping off alone to the Nissen hut in which the party was to be held. The fabric dragged carelessly round her shoulders was more like a Basuto pony blanket than a stole, her tough tweed skirt scraped against the gravel path as she swung along, head afloat.

In the distance friends of the group looked like tiny black pins in the lighted doorway of the hut. Dick and Victor and I and several others walked towards it, frost glinted obscenely beside the path. We all started to walk faster. Inside the hut everyone was chattering at the same time to keep warm. Victor and I collected drinks from the bar and handed them round.

'I bet you all need this,' said Dick, who was the host.

Someone toasted the show.

'May it run forever!'

'My God, that tenor's got a magnificent voice.'

Margaret was perched on a desk talking abstractedly to the lady novelist. The hut smelled of chemistry tutorials. A small cheer went up as the tenor burst in with a shiny face.

People drank fast and rather nervously. 'There's Hazel,' I said to Victor.

He turned away swiftly and I lost sight of him.

A woman in amber serge said, 'The most exciting night in the theatre in years. Do we know each other?'

Our names flew away unheard. 'How do you think the critics will like it?'

'Doesn't matter. Everything's above their heads apart from Rodgers and Hammerstein.'

Victor hopped jokingly from group to group, I had never known him so expansive before. He was a spectacular sight in his hired dinner jacket. Next to him all the other men looked like wisps of smoke. I had taken his measurements to a shop that hired out fancy dress costumes because there was nowhere he could go himself. I told the sour-mouthed owner the suit was for my uncle from Cincinnati. I took my parcel with an unasked for feeling of triumph at having hired for a black man a suit that would be worn next week by a white one.

All sorts of people flashed this way and that and for a second or two I was on my own, my mind a complete blank. Nearby Len Silver dropped on to a desk within an inch of an inkwell. I pictured him driving refugees in the boot of his car to the Swazi border on moonless nights. Once in Swaziland what did the refugees do next? When I caught his eye he made the thumbs up sign.

He came over to say, 'Nobody gives a stuff about the sets,' but he was smiling cheerfully enough.

'Who cares? We like them.'

He steered a knotty squint-eyed girl into a corner and kept his back to the room.

Victor came up from behind me. 'Talk about the life and soul,' I said. I was delighted he was making his own way with so little effort.

'It's fun, hey. Having fun?'

Then I noticed the strange tic at the sides of his eyes and I knew he was under some strain or other.

I made myself smile to hide the discovery. 'Drink?'

'On my third. Quite a party.'

'Dick knows how to make things go. You wouldn't think so

when you first meet him.'

'You want to stay long?'

'Haven't spoken to any of the cast yet.' I wondered what reason there could be for Victor's uneasiness.

He laughed under his breath. 'Haven't you seen enough of them lately?'

'The least we can do is congratulate them. Did you think it flopped?'

Victor shrugged, rubbing his hand against his empty glass. 'The show's fine. Maybe I've seen too much of it.'

Bared teeth in white faces surrounded the stars of the show, the chorus crowded together on benches against the wall. Out of costume they looked terribly ordinary and rather apologetic. They had jobs to get to in the morning and seemed concerned about this.

I said, 'We don't have to stay if you don't want to.'

But already Hazel had slipped in alongside us. 'Well, of all the no-good stuck-up – '

'Hazel, you've made it,' I said.

Victor took a long time about turning towards her. Eventually he said, 'It was your night, everyone says so.'

'Hazel, you're a star. Does it feel different?' I wanted a tone as light as air, but it wouldn't come.

'You really think it was all right?'

I nodded till I had to make myself stop. 'Your shebeen scene – the crowd would've let it go on all night.'

'I play it another way now, you notice? Last time you two showed up at rehearsal it wasn't like this.' Her eyes flicked from me to Victor, then back to me. 'So tell me, where you been lately?'

'Around. Where else?'

Hazel's laugh darted in a little too fast. 'Don't ask me. I'm in the dark.'

Voices crashed and banged on all sides and the three of us waited for someone to speak.

Hazel faced up to Victor. 'They say you've moved from

your friends' place.'

Victor was all smiles. 'Who says?'

'Never mind. I got ears.'

'Lekker ones too.'

'*You* should care!'

'Can I get you a drink?' I said to Hazel.

No answer. She wasn't herself tonight, she was like a quick stinging snake.

She's overtired, she's living on her nerves. Everyone's so odd tonight something's going to blow up if we don't watch out.

She said to Victor, 'Man alive, we folks miss you now you've gone over to the other side.'

'Come on, Hazel, play the game.' Victor's very still cool voice came like thunder.

I didn't know this world, the code was beyond me.

And then there was Hazel's soft mocking style. 'You tell me the game, I'll play it.'

'I've moved away meanwhile. Nothing to bother about.'

'I sincerely hope not. You know how folks talk and what can a person do about it?'

'But you're not the talking type. We're old pals, hey. You won't let us down.'

Yes, definitely a plea here. How unlike the Victor I knew, or perhaps my conception of him, and immediately I saw everything with different eyes.

You had to strain to catch Hazel's whisper. 'So it's *us*. That what you said?'

Their day-to-day life is made up of shifting sands. They're used to it. I don't understand the way they taunt each other, and yet stick together in the end. 'Please, Hazel, forget about it,' I butted in.

She appeared to slacken off. 'Sure,' she said. 'Just put it down to curiosity. So damn little to talk about these days.'

The icy air outside was like fire in my throat. But the shakes that rippled through me from head to foot came from fear. Or was it release from fear? On the hook one minute, let off the next. Anyhow Victor grabbed my elbow as we staggered up the path.

'Don't worry. Treat it as a joke,' he said.

'Some joke. What the hell got into her tonight?'

'Forget it, we're going home. In twenty minutes we'll be home. Now isn't that a nice thought?'

'But I want to know.'

Victor sighed – a long weird sound dragged up from the gut. 'Ag, how can I put it? You're a kid and you're white and why should you trouble yourself about all this shit?'

'It's sort of envy with Hazel, isn't it? A person must be terribly unhappy to take an attitude like that.'

'Ja, envy comes into it, why not? And where does the envy come from? Call it frustration. Not the sort of frustration you talk about when you've been held up in a traffic jam on your way to work or when you can't get an outside line because the switchboard's overloaded. It's more than that, I can tell you. Nothing changes, nothing will ever change. No light anywhere. To talk about hope ... well, that's just laughable. And you get sick of laughing, and then you're just plain sick. Hazel's a star tonight, but how much does that count for in the street tomorrow? She's just another nigger girl carrying a pass.'

We shot into the car and I started the engine and switched on the heater all in one movement. We drove away from the Corinthian columns into the main highway with its chilly blue overhead lights.

Victor said, 'You see, in a way, I've broken out. I'm not in the township where I ought to be, according to the law, and this gets under people's skins. Their curiosity won't let them alone. They're fascinated and angry and wish me luck all in one breath.'

'We've just got to be more careful,' I said.

I simply shut my mind to the misery he was talking about. Just to get over the moment. This was all that life was made up of. One had to. It was a question of carrying on. My desire for survival drove out everything else. Let Hazel and the others find *their* way out. Victor had found his. Up to a point. I would fight tooth and nail to – Who was the poet who claimed he'd murder his own mother if necessary? That a sonnet is worth any number of old ladies?

I said, 'If we're sensible and don't take risks we can still have a good life and everything will be all right.'

Victor was whistling to himself, I knew his mind was turning over with conflicting thoughts. Then he said, 'I've broken a promise. I wish I hadn't. Right at the beginning I promised myself I would never bring up this subject and I would never let you draw me out on it.'

'But you can't make arrangements with yourself like that. It's like cheating.'

'I didn't see it like that. It seemed to me to be more positive than that. Something I could do for you, or give you, like a present.'

He seemed so disappointed I wanted to say something to take him out of himself or at least to make him laugh, but nothing worthwhile came to mind and one couldn't insult him with second best.

After a while he said, 'Anyway the promise is broken, so there we are, what can we do about it?'

I'll shut the damned world out. But this was nonsense of course, it was Saturday, there was the shopping to do. And when you are young how quickly you put setbacks behind you, spring up again after blows. There is a pliancy, then, that simply disappears one day, its place being taken by a heart that is forever running away. Once I got to the shops an amusement park atmosphere came to life.

The shopping centre glistened with crimson cars out of which lacquered young women in bright bulky sweaters and skinny jeans and suede boots slithered swinging ignition keys on their fingers. I could have saved us money by shopping in a less smart suburb but I reasoned what the hell, let's eat the best, the movies and the ballet and the ice rink and just about everything else you can name is out of bounds for us.

We shared expenses, up to a point. My salary was higher than Victor's which was a shameful state of affairs, considering his age and experience and the hard grind forced upon him. We never discussed this, pride was at stake. Between us stretched a no-man's-land on which it was better not to trespass. My past, or upbringing, whatever you like to call it, is always close at hand calling the tune. Because I can't shake it off, I suppose. Victor's didn't matter to him, or so he made out after long training. I think he would have talked about it if it had been happy, or if it had any parallel with my own, but how could it? So he pretended he could discount it.

I simply cashed another cheque when I decided we should have prawns and fillet and Nederburg Cuvée Brut. Barely making it from month to month corresponded most appropriately with the way of life we were obliged to lead.

By now my secret had become second nature to me. At certain times in public, say, in the supermarket or the Belgian confectioner's, the sights around me would spark off an intense awareness of it. My malformed but favourite child, who requires constant protection from the world outside, is given a pat on the shoulder, as it were. Among the imported cheeses the stockbroker's deliberately pale young wife was fencing with someone who bored her. 'Madrid? Oh quite good for bags. But thank heavens for Milan.' 'Must let you in on a little secret. The place for poodle collars is Brussels.' 'We only go to Brussels to eat.' I dropped some Brie into my basket.

I drove home under the bare trees. Victor had sold his car, there was no alternative. The sight of him driving out each morning and returning in the evening would have had the neighbourhood on our tracks within a week. It was safer for him to take the bus from Jan Smuts Avenue, around the corner. His buses were always full, he was soon lost in the crowd. To reach the stop he trotted down the sanitary lane that ran from the bottom of our garden to the main road. An eerie tunnel of a lane that smelled of roots and mould, invariably deserted. When his hours coincided with mine we drove into town together and I brought him home afterwards. As long as we didn't make a habit of this no one would be able to read anything into it, we considered.

The stuffy little khaya in the backyard was where he slept, 'officially'. Meticulously soiled sheets were on the bed and some of his clothes hung in the pine-wood cupboard. Once a week I went inside to dust the room and change the cigarette butts in the ashtray. I kept three or four cigarette butts for this purpose.

I hate going into that room, and Victor knows this, so I make a point of timing my weekly visit when he is away at work. The cypress hedge leans bang up against the window blocking out the light. I leave it that way, I am an employer, I do what I like. I dent the pillow, push shoes around, swivel the feather duster here and there, try to ignore the houseboy's calico uniform hanging from a hook behind the door. Next step is the lavatory and the shower. I slosh water over the floor and dampen the soap. How cosy, how lived in. In the end I am pleased with my work and reckon I would be a spy not to be trifled with in any war they might care to name.

I try to picture the room through the eyes of an outsider seeing it for the first time. The appearance of the room must always smack of occupation. Yes, sergeant, this is the boy's room. Yes, he has a pass to work in this area. Today's his day off. One day off a week and every second Sunday, the usual thing. No, never have any trouble with him, he's the quiet type, hold thumbs. Doesn't drink, no women hanging round. Miskien is hy a moffie. Haha. You should be in the circus, sergeant. Whoever heard of a queer kaffir anyway? Stick to the well-worn path that forges a link between house owner and sergeant. Be brutally offhand (don't stop halfway) and the two of you are brothers striking common ground together. Which is crucial for Victor and me. We want top marks in the sergeant's end of term report.

I drove into the garage, glad to be home, and carried my parcels through to the kitchen and began putting things away. It was one of those old-fashioned kitchens with chocolate brown walls, chipped linoleum both on the floor and on the table, an ancient refrigerator that barked like a grumpy dog, a wire-mesh meat safe of the type found in the ramshackle beach cottages we spent our holidays in as children. 'Unhygienic,' my mother used to snap, summer after summer. I could have spent hours on end in the kitchen perfectly content.

'Victor.'

From the kitchen window, which needed cleaning, I watched him on his haunches in the garden and I stopped what I was doing, unable to resist the compulsion to talk to him again, and went outside. Was it some deep down desire that perhaps even he himself did not acknowledge that made him reshape the soil of this white man's garden? Almost a proprietary air about him bending over that fork ...

'Look,' he said, 'do you know what it is?'

I stared into it, perplexed.

'No,' he said, 'it is not a grave.'

'What is it then?'

'A trench for sweet peas. We're going to have sweet peas, you watch.'

'Isn't it a bit late for sweet peas?'

'Ours will be out when everyone else's are over.'

'You're a very fast digger.'

'Suddenly got the urge. What I know about gardening is dangerous, so don't get too excited.'

'Here's our pudding for tonight.'

I opened a neat baker's box full of brandy snaps and rum babas. Victor took a rum baba and put it in his mouth.

'It's for tonight,' I said.

'It's terrific. What are the others?'

We settled down on the spiky beige lawn and polished off all the rum babas and half the brandy snaps, I had never tasted better. Food. Question mark. Though Victor accepted what

I dished up, I wondered whether regular meals were of any importance to him. Having got by on his own for so long, did he consider a chop and two veg an infliction? Or a chain round his foot perhaps? Or did it not register at all that one hot meal followed another in disciplined procession?

'Did you like being married?' I said.

'It had its moments.'

'How many?'

'Two,' he laughed.

'Which two?'

'Of no consequence any more.'

'Why did you get married?' I asked.

'It was the fashion at the time. We were all young and pals together and we had our first proper jobs and then everyone started getting married, so I joined the bandwaggon. Didn't think about it too much. Just met a pretty girl and got married.'

'Dolores.'

'Uh-huh.'

'I asked Hazel about her.'

'That so?'

'But if you knew about yourself, and don't tell me you didn't, why did you get married? Why didn't you team up with some other guy and settle down with him, like us?'

Victor smiled, and he could smile very charmingly when he felt like it. 'That tradition doesn't seem to have really taken root among Zulus.'

'Zulus are crazy.'

'You sometimes find uncles seducing their nephews if there are no women to be had.'

'That's not what I'm talking about. That happens in Arkansas or anywhere.'

'Arkansas?'

'Listen,' I said, 'the next time you go to visit your daughter don't you think I should come along too?'

'Sure. Please yourself,' he said.

2

'Tonight? We can't. We've got to go to this party for this Cape opera group.'

'Opera? ... from the *Cape*?'

'This Coloured group. The papers have been full of it, don't you read?'

'Nobody told me about this party, where is it?'

'When we were at this mine opening in the Free State this week the Stanfords asked us.'

'Oh you and those softy liberals. The richer they are the more they fall about whenever a darkie raises himself above the cotton pickin' stage.'

'Not these – '

'And whether they're liberal or not the local aristocracy are as much fun as gala night at the automat.'

'The Stanfords are different. Victor gets on with them too. Dick admires Victor, I'm not joking.'

'Mother of mercy, why on earth should you?'

'If you knew them you'd know what I mean.'

Frankie sniffed. 'What the uppercrust does to me is straight out of *Dracula*. But what *I* do to *them*. Honey, I can turn a mild old marquess into a mass murderer by the merest gesture – like maybe leaning on his lunch on the way back to the drawing room.'

'Go on, everyone likes you.'

Frankie's hands flew up in front of his mischievous monkey's face. 'The way they show it!'

'We hardly ever go out. Can't you put off your party till next week?'

'These dolls will be gone by then. They've just blown in from Bulawayo. In sackcloth, need I add? These Rhodesian broads – where do they *find* these frocks?'

'Oh well, don't forget us next time.' I pretended to be tying the laces of my tennis shoes. I stared down at the ants whizzing through the grass between my legs. I jumped up to shout, 'What's the score, ninety-all or something?'

On the court Geoff held up his fingers. Four-three, it looked like.

'Victor's really chasing him today,' I said.

'Honeybear.'

The expression on Frankie's face was so earnest I knew what was coming.

'I'm forgiven, am I?'

'I never gave it another thought.'

'That makes you some kind of saint. When it comes back at me – what I said to you – I wake up screaming. The shock – you gave me a shock, you know. I always make a scene when I'm kicked in the cunt. Once I got to live with the idea it made sense.'

'Did it? Love and sense don't usually go together. I've never thought about it as being sensible. I love him more than anybody else, that's all it amounts to.'

Frankie put a vague hand on my knee, which he then rat-a-tat-tatted with the tips of his nails. He treated his nails with some sort of solution to keep them from splitting.

'Anyhow, when I look around here and see how happy you've made him, what can one add but "May your union be blessed with issue"?'

'We get on well together, nothing else to it. They've finished.' I bolted. The sun was hot for August. 'What happened in the end?'

'He did it again. Six-four,' Victor said.

'What you lack is staying power,' and I threw him his jersey.

'Come on, Frankie. I'm going to donner you.'

Frankie groaned. 'I'm too wan for singles. Why can't they make tennis eleven a side, like in football?'

It was as I threw up the ball to serve that a flash of light – but is it light? – nicked my eye. Double fault.

'Love-fifteen. I'm leading,' Frankie cried.

I looked left, towards the cypress hedge. I peered at the frowsty surface of the hedge. The surface was blurred in one spot, as though the hedge were balding, letting through the light from the next door garden. I stepped nearer, where a ball was lying. In the depths of the hedge I made out a child's face. A tiny girl with buttery hair, I couldn't even guess at her age. How long has she been hiding there? Victor. Victor was now in the shade of a tree on the other side of the court. I smiled at the child, I did not speak to her. As long as no one else knows we're being watched … With deliberate abruptness I bent to pick up the ball. The child's face vanished. Only a very faint whirring of branches could be heard.

Again a double fault.

Frankie was chuckling to himself. 'They told me I'd drawn Billie Jean. By the way, whatever happened to Billie Jean?'

'You've had your handicap. Now we start.'

He had no strokes to speak of, merely persistence. He batted back every ball he could get to. Even though I had often set out to do so I had never been able to beat him 6-0. Back came the ball, and back and back, until you smashed it into the net in exasperation, immediately regretted. This delighted Frankie, he duck-walked his way back to the baseline to wait for my next mistake.

The child would be at tea by now. Animal biscuits and cube sugar? Would her parents listen to what she had to tell them? On the other hand, perhaps she was a child who kept her secrets to herself. The sweat broke out in my armpits, I couldn't control it. But can a child interpret what it has seen?

I put over a sneaky little drop shot and Frankie stamped his foot and glared at the ball, hissing 'I hate you,' and we went off the court under the deodar tree. You could tell it was a long way from summer, in the shade there was still winter in the air.

I ran into the house to put the kettle on. Cups slipped out of my hands on to the tray, it was like gunfire in my ears. I steadied myself as I tipped the chocolate cake from its tin on to a plate.

Victor came in to carry things outside and I failed to keep the snap out of my voice. 'For Christ's sake put your jersey on. Who's going to nurse you through pneumonia?' A look of surprise crossed his face as he backed out with the tray.

We lounged on the lawn in the sunshine drinking tea and they ate up most of the chocolate cake and my sense of foreboding shifted away a bit and I began to join in the conversation again. Frankie and Victor picked up their rackets. Geoff wanted to take the tea things back to the kitchen.

'Leave them, there's lots of time. What can we do about Victor's sweet peas? They've got mange if you ask me.'

We strolled around the garden. Neither of us was afraid of silence. Geoff's legs were unnaturally thin, I think he must have had some vicious illness as a child, though the subject was never brought up. The rest of his body seemed to have escaped it. In fact he had every right to be proud of his chest, which billowed out beneath beautiful coat hanger shoulders. Greying hair at the sides of his head did not seem a cliché with him, one couldn't visualise it ever having been different. His rather melancholy blue eyes suited his voice, in which it was virtually impossible to detect an inflection. Good in the operating theatre more than likely. The scalpel, nurse. Now the saw. I thought the back of his head needed more of a bump to it, it was too close to being a single plane, like a cliff face the wrong way round.

'Here we have a lasiandra,' he said. 'Doesn't like frost. That's a petrea.'

'Everything looks much the same at the end of winter.'

'You are lucky. This is a white bauhinia.'

We rounded the corner of the house, the sun was behind it.

'Gardening's a good way of unwinding. I probably wouldn't

set foot in ours if it wasn't. Frankie has a curious attitude to flowers. He can recognise an orchid, but only when it's on someone's shoulder.'

Geoff bent closer to a rose bush. Funny, white men left me cold these days. They looked like paper cut-outs, for one thing. You can't depend on a piece of paper, it has neither fibre nor blood. As for fire – well, paper goes up in smoke at the faintest touch of it. Yes, I like the fire, I think life must be awfully thin going if you don't. But quite apart from the fire. Or perhaps beyond it would be more precise. Whereas a flame can't be. And, strange to say, there is a rock force as well. Old old rocks. Yet not foreign. At least I didn't find them so. After Victor, I'd be an appalling flop with a white man. I met this eunuch, he'd say the next day. I wasn't always like this. At school, for instance. Oh the usual hand stuff. Quite a lot of it, as a matter of fact. But it was as though one were merely fidgeting round the edges, not reaching the core. The central need that only crystallised later on in life.

'Whoever pruned these roses deserves to have the secateur turned on himself.'

I came to slowly, though not unwillingly. 'Wasn't there a movie that started off with a body in the rose garden?'

Geoff and I smiled across at each other, the shade was deepening with every minute.

'Ray, should there ever be anything you find you can't cope with, you will let me know, won't you?'

A quick little spasm went right through me. So he did see that damned child. *He* saw her.

'I've wondered sometimes what we'd do if Victor got ill. A burst appendix or something. I'd fuck the lot of them if he had to go into that Baragwanath hospital. Would they let me visit him?'

Geoff swerved away to laugh, which was a habit of his. 'If it was a burst appendix I'm afraid he'd be whipped into Baragwanath whether you fucked the lot of them or not.'

'Well, flu then. Like that Asian flu. Would you come round

and examine him and tell me which antibiotics to get?'

'I think I might.'

'That's a load off my mind!' and I worked up a mock shiver and started backing away out of the shadow of the house.

'But it wasn't illness I was talking about. I've always taken it for granted you'd call me in.'

'Yes ... of course.'

I retraced my steps to hear the rest of it.

I said, 'I'm sorry if I seemed rude, you're the last person I would – '

'It mightn't always be plain sailing for you and Victor. Obviously you realise this. If any difficulty crops up don't think you have to face it on your own. I'd be hurt if you didn't come to me first.'

'Thanks.' Then I said, 'Why did you ... I mean, is there any particular reason why you brought this up now?'

'I've been wanting to speak to you for ages. Never get a chance with Frankie around.'

Only I knew. It was better that way, yet I felt very alone all of a sudden. Could that child be back at the hedge? But I wouldn't even bother to look. By not looking I might expel her forever.

'Thanks, Geoff. We wouldn't stand a chance without our friends.'

Cold lemony sunlight lay on the needles of the deodar tree, half the court was in shadow and the tramlines needed repainting. I made up my mind to remember the names of the shrubs in the garden. Now, that's a petrea, it has mauve flowers. I dipped my head to see if any buds were coming through.

Frankie and Victor seemed to surround us.

'We've got a white bauhinia,' I said.

'It's so vulgar to have coloured flowers,' Frankie said.

He and Geoff were soon laden with coats and jerseys and rackets.

Frankie said, 'I must go fling some oreganum into the pot

luck.'

'What're you giving them to eat?' I asked.

'I've just told you.'

'If the Stanford party falls flat, come over to us,' Geoff said.

'That's an idea,' I said. I liked him more than ever.

'You're just being tactful. You don't have to be tactful with me,' Margaret said. 'Let's go up to the studio,' she said, 'they can look after themselves for a bit.'

The copper and iron rail alone had cost Dick a thousand pounds. Staff at the office knew all about it, they loved gossiping about the directors' wives. People whose tastes were different to Margaret's, which meant nearly everyone she came into contact with, said, 'Poor Dick, he lets her get away with murder.' It was an outside staircase, you reached it from the garden. A metalworker whom Margaret had discovered in a shed in the garment district had designed the rail for her. She stroked it protectively as we went up the staircase under the moon. When she had switched on the light she jumped on to a daybed among stubby black and brown cushions.

'Take all the others,' she went on. 'Lorna St David, Juliet Park, Sue Gordon-Brown. Without the least sign of effort they never put a foot wrong. And then you get Marianne Langenvelder. She's in a class of her own. But I suppose chairmen's wives *have* to be. That's why chairmen marry them. Did you notice her at that deadly mine opening on Wednesday? She sailed through it without turning a hair. The impression she creates is so terribly *right*.'

Abruptly Margaret ripped down her own hair to make a wimple. If only she didn't mind being thought of as a clown. By conscientiously putting her mind to it she could have been a wonderful clown. But she chose to direct her honesty into solemn fields and failed almost totally. Her output was small, the choice of subject itself being a dilemma she could rarely sort out on her own. Books and odds and ends seemed to have been deliberately placed so as to partly conceal the three or four of her sculptures on the studio shelves. Neither form nor texture held one's eye for long.

'You know, if I hadn't married Dick I'd have gone the whole hog and been a bohemian. Nothing more exasperating than being neither one thing nor the other. Have you made up your mind about yourself?'

'Yes,' I said, 'I think so.'

'Congratulations. And don't be a fool. Marry a girl whom everyone else praises to the skies. You'll be off to a good start.'

'Dick's mad about you. The masses don't have an opinion anyway.'

Margaret leapt up, she left her hair to hang down just as it was. 'The thing to do is to keep both your feet in one camp. There's a constant gnawing inside you if you don't. Bad for the pancreas!' She shrugged, but without resignation.

'Do you think they're enjoying themselves downstairs? My parties always fall between a dozen stools.'

From the door of the studio you saw only the sky at first. Then its impact altered a little as the scent of carnations rose from the garden.

'Why do we have these parties? Are we so conscience-struck that we're too afraid not to? Yet now and then you meet someone you'd like to see again. Your friend Victor, for instance. There he is – one can get down to things with him. On the whole it's like yelling across a void. Alternatively everyone gets dead drunk and there's no need to. Dick says one mustn't give up though.'

Margaret plunged into the sitting room, the baritone caught hold of my elbow and drove me across the terrace. We kept on half missing the steps that curved down on to the lawn but somehow we found our balance again just in time.

'What I need is a drink. You've probably had ten already,' I said.

'You aren't surprised, are you? I can tell you're not

surprised.'

I asked him his name, I never catch names when introductions are made.

'Is that your stage name or your real name?'

He was a man of many parts, he said.

He found a bench under an apricot tree. Stringy branches hid most of the stars and the leaves of arum lilies brushed against me. Margaret's mermaid fountain burped in the darkness somewhere. The baritone was fairly high but not drunk.

'That guy's your beau, hey. The minute you walked in it stood out a mile. You been together long? Don't tell me you stick by the sixth commandment.'

He took my hand and put it on his leg. 'Hello handful, don't you ever come down to Cape Town?' His tongue wiggled between my lips. The brandy in his mouth was mixed with a greasepaint smell, it reminded me of incense foaming out of the thurible at Benediction.

'Relax, child. You Joburg children never relax.'

There was a gentleness about him, clearly decipherable behind the bulldozing technique. 'A quickie,' he murmured, 'lovely lovely quick quick quick.' He was fiddling with his zip and I thought, Jesus Christ, in Dick's garden of all gardens. And Geoff had said, if the Stanford party falls flat ...

'On the invitation card it didn't say this was a surprise party,' I said.

'You have such beautiful thoughts.'

'Anyhow,' I said, 'what's so great about Cape Town?'

'It isn't called the Mother City on account of a lot of old Nellies in wheelchairs. We know how to live,' he said.

'How do you live?'

'Don't talk so much. Aren't I black enough for you?'

He started chewing the lobe of an ear. I looked over his head into a dark border which might very well have been phlox. Someone I knew once had sex on a park bench while the band played a medley from *Brigadoon*.

'You're too tense,' he said, and I thought, those must be

the most often repeated words in the world, especially on a Saturday night.

'The weather,' I said.

'What's the weather got to do with us being happy?' and he played his next card, shoved my hand inside his pants.

I managed to stand up, leaving him intact.

'What's wrong?'

'Nothing, only that – '

'So? No one's ever complained about the size before.'

'I'm not complaining,' I said.

He stayed moodily on the bench. I walked away after a while.

'The shape's okay too,' he hissed.

Among all those faces in the too brightly lit room I picked out Victor's straight away. I was a perfect target in the French windows, he had only to swivel his eyes a fraction to see me, which is what he did. He and Dick were talking solemnly together. He made no sign that I should join them. I made my way towards the people next to them, they smiled shyly at me. Even without the bands of black liner the soprano's eyes would have filled up her face. No, I hadn't seen *Traviata*, I told her, but everyone was ecstatic about her Violetta. She was pleased, she said, it was her favourite role. Followed by? I asked.

Behind me Dick was saying to Victor, 'How did it go off in the Free State? Did you get all the material you wanted?'

'Ray had it all laid on. Not a hitch. He's a born organiser.'

'That's what they all tell me, I'm glad to hear it.'

'Those mine people can be difficult if they want to. But he didn't give them a chance. Had them eating out of his hand.'

'Splendid. I suppose you get it everywhere ... this suspicion of head office. The mines are quite convinced that nothing goes on at head office but long lunches and a lot of hot air. Heaven knows how one changes their minds. You got back last night?'

'Six on the dot. In spite of a flat tyre just outside Kroonstad.'

'Damned nuisance on a long trip. How's your drink?'

Yes, we had seats for *Bohème*, I lied to the soprano.

Victor isn't allowed in, I should have told her.

Johannesburg audiences were wonderful, she said.

Across ranks of heads I spotted the baritone smiling cheerfully at me and I felt absolved. Till Mimi, I told the soprano, and pushed through to him. The cast filled Margaret's sitting room like a flock of bright plumaged birds. They rustled and trilled and clinked wine glasses with Margaret's friends, many of whom were professionally adapted to making small talk with guests who weren't white. How wan we whites must look, yet the balance is nicely struck. One blonde for each brunette. Coffee skins, tea skins, soup skins, all of them with a waxy sheen. A honeyish powder smell came across in trickles, then waves. The room was strawberry coloured. Gashes of mustard here and there. By fixing your eye to details you could pick out blackened masks and a pregnant torso in bronze, yards of abstracts in slime green and grass green, a silver urn crammed with larkspurs.

'Here's a brandy,' the baritone said.

'Thanks.'

He lifted his glass. 'Nice knowing you. See you in Cape Town one day.'

'Sorry about just now.'

'Not to worry. I went ahead on my own anyway.' He laughed into his glass. 'Was my pass too forward? I'll try anything once. We Coloureds are the randiest people on earth, didn't you know that?'

The sooty bruises under his eyes almost concealed the tiny creases in the skin. But he would never brood, he would dress up and stride out and break into action for as long as his balls could take it.

I said, 'I'm glad you didn't stay outside the rest of the night.'

'Jesus, how long does it take you to – '

Margaret whisked him away to meet a deathly pale couple

in a corner.

Victor appeared out of the blue to say, 'Are we off?'

'What's the time?'

'The party's breaking up, you can feel it.'

'What a mad party. I've hardly had a thing to drink.'

'I'm not surprised. You can't fit in everything.'

A chilly tone, words spat out like stones. I stared at him for a long time. The pinched look round his mouth bewildered me.

'What are you saying – or trying not to? Use words of one syllable, then maybe I'll understand.'

He shook his head. 'Do you want one for the road?' he said.

'Perhaps I'd better not,' I said and put down my glass.

'You might as well know it. I'm driving,' he said.

'Are you?'

We found Dick, then Margaret. Good night, great party. Victor's fist on my spine kept me moving. I was ill-tempered and afraid. I seemed incapable of holding on to a single state of mind, each one alternating every few seconds. I stalked ahead down the road past cars glinting under the street lamps like prize slugs and slopped into the passenger seat. Victor took the keys.

'Don't you do that again, I'm warning you,' he said.

'Do what, I didn't do a damn thing,' I said.

He chivvied the engine feverishly, we roared down the deserted road.

'You lousy driver,' I said.

'What the hell was going on outside?' he said.

Just behave yourself in future, he said. Whether he knew about it or didn't know – this didn't come into it. He made no room for subtleties, he said. If I cheated him with someone else, don't worry, he'd soon find out. He'd beat me up till I wouldn't know what day of the week it was. Who did I think *I* was – and *he* was? What gave me the idea I could do whatever I liked with whoever took my fancy. That broken

72

down half-caste from District Six. Was he nice, he asked, was it big? Who sucked who? Or was it a joint effort? And neither of you bothered to cover up, he laughed sourly. Even drank a toast to it. Or was that just to rinse your mouths out? In front of everyone, the fucking nerve of it. You try it again, he said, you won't forget it. You won't look so pretty any more, people will run a mile when they see you, I promise you.

'He got fresh but nothing happened,' I said.

Ha ha, he'd heard that one before.

'I tried to put him off but it took time,' I said.

'Sure. Half an hour.'

'It wasn't half an hour,' I said.

'What I can't stand about you is your superiority. You've got a sense of superiority second to none. And that's saying something when you take into account the statistics. Those three million others made of the same sort of crap as you. Tell me something,' he said, 'I'm interested.'

He changed gears. There was no need to, but he had to do something with his hands. The engine bellowed in second gear.

He said, 'Would you fuck with a black man in, say, England? Or wouldn't it have the same kick there? Maybe in England you'd make out with the cripples or the deaf mutes.'

At last he changed down to third again.

'No,' he said, 'those poor black buggers in England are losers. You've got to be black right here in the fatherland for certain people to come running. We blacks have all the luck, hey? Boy, how those white kids spread for us. Like bitches on heat. Only there's a difference. The bitches on heat here are cold as ice underneath.'

I lit a cigarette, dropping matches all over the seat. I scratched about in the stitching of the seat trying to pick them up.

Victor said, 'Why did you go after me in the first place? To raise your own value in the market? Must be plenty of old kinkies would pay the earth for someone who's tasted black.'

'Otherwise,' I said, 'how did you enjoy the party? Or have I already asked you?'

'Shut up. I'm for honest,' he said. 'I play it straight. You're a mess. You're full of tricks.'

'Honest people are a bore. There's nothing to them. Just their honesty.'

'Always thought there must be something crooked behind that front you put up. Don't flap around me any more, see?'

'Probably won't have the time anyhow, so that fixes that.'

'Just stop flapping around me, I don't need it.'

I said, 'You know it yourself, but I might as well let you know that I know. Ready?'

'You and your superior shit.'

'The fact is, you're disappointed in yourself. You couldn't hold your wife. Now you're beginning to see you can't hold me either.'

'Negative arguments don't impress me. You don't stand a chance against me with a negative argument.'

'Your disappointment doesn't end there of course. You want to be the strong man. Because you think you should be. And because you think *I* think you should be. But you can't carry it off, you haven't got it in you.'

'You certainly know how to show yourself up as a weakling.'

Victor flashed through a yellow light, I waited for the siren to sound. Let them catch us, it'll clear the air. Something outside ourselves to put full stop to war. War is primitive and boring. Doesn't even settle the nerves.

'Smoke?'

No answer. Obviously not. In the silence worry took over again. Not about what had happened, nor about what might still happen later on tonight, but about tomorrow, after we had slept it off. No precedent to guide me in judging how one picked up the old threads again in the morning. Nothing behind us to refer to. This, to me, had seemed an advantage in the beginning. A clean slate on which to start, everything spanking new. It was up to us, exclusively, to make something out of it. But doubts flocking in now. Victor was a stranger to me, he did not think or feel as I did.

Our trains of thought must be running in the same direction at the same time. The only difference, however, is the drivers themselves.

'I'll open the gate,' I said.

'Stay where you are. You might try and run back to that cocksucking opera singer. It's my turn now.'

And so on, without raising our voices.

I shrugged and told him, 'Please yourself.'

'I intend to,' he said.

Haven't seen you for ages, my mother wrote. Surprise! we're thinking of coming up now the winter's over. You know what Daddy thinks of Johannesburg. Me too for that matter. How can you possibly approve of it? And don't say I'm anti-Semitic! This house of yours – can't make it out. Who cooks for you and who does the laundry? Your letters so vague they might as well come from the moon. Are you sharing with two others – or twenty? Fun having a court. Wish you'd take it up seriously again. And what's happened to your squash? You mustn't let things slide, darling. Daddy's well, he works too hard. A great compliment passed at the side-bar dinner last night. Daddy has the best legal brain in the country. Who said so? No less than the guest of honour, Judge Viljoen from the Appellate Division! I was next to him, he's a poppet. The Country Club did it superbly. Am without a cook again, I could scream, and it's not as though they're underpaid these days, not on your life …

Office planning send me on tour of group properties suggest visit later in year alternatively expect me for Xmas writing love.

I sent off the telegram from the greasy little post office at the far end of Commissioner Street where I parked the car in the mornings. Cities anywhere have these tattered districts on the edge of midtown. In South Africa they bear a common stamp: whites simply don't go there, except in their cars, passing through. A kind of bogeyman's land. To visitors, people brag in reverse, as it were – they'd slit your throat for sixpence, I'm telling you. Gangs by the score, no exaggeration. They come at you out of nowhere. And don't think passers-by in the street are any protection. They even operate in the peak hour these days, the rest of the mob just steps over you. The worst day is Friday, payday, any time from 5 pm on.

This wariness once existed in me no less than in anyone else. Even in my subdued home town we knew (no one actually told us, as far as I remember) that in some way the streets by the river were out of bounds. Oddly enough, living with Victor flushed this particular inheritance out of me. Gradually at first, while the influence of our life together gathered pace.

The racket is deafening. It is made up of voices looping breathlessly from one uncanny pitch to another, unlike the midtown sounds which come from car hooters and brakes. Apart from the police station, Central Square, no building is more than two storeys high and, though not old, they all look second-hand, as though picked up at auction marts. Smoking cans in alleys and the glare of a bronze sari vanishing into a lopsided doorway and the Omo girl in the shop entrance patting her straightened hair before getting down to the day's work of converting every passer-by into a customer. KwaDabulamanzi. This is the sign over the herbalist's den crammed with roots and bark and old jamjars mysteriously half-filled with either crimson or electric blue powder. Next door the notice in the window of the Chinese restaurant says 'No waiters needed, do not apply' and a three-and-a-half-legged cat stumps into the dirty puddle of sunlight in front of it.

Central Square is new and antiseptic and strikes a scary note in this area. It heaps itself towards the sky without style or grace. The wall-cladding is a bright scrubbed green and catches the sun. Did an architect from Public Works read in a thesis that prisoners are more likely to loosen up in a building with a supermarket facade? But, then, what was it like inside? Once a prisoner had broken away from his interrogators to throw himself from the top storey, lit up by the setting sun as he fell past the green cladding to the pavement. Someone from a newspaper took a picture, for which he won a prize.

The Indians own the shops and their customers are Africans. There are many more Africans in the city than all the other races put together.

They no longer roll towards me as a single black wave. The faces approach individually, my eye is alive, now, to variations in plane, shade, depth. In the early evening the leisurely air is gone. Danger time. Though queues push into liquor stores, most people are storming up the pavements towards buses and trains. I look up into the faded sky but I lose my footing and make a grab at the parcel I have dropped and bob along in the crush. Perhaps Victor is waiting at the car, more often not. He has taken an early bus or will arrive home on a later one.

It is growing darker by the minute, quite definitely I feel a bond between these people and me. Is the reverse of this feeling what happens to me among white strangers nowadays? Like when I was shopping at Stuttaford's last week and the tidy little voice crooned 'Cash or entry, sir?' I don't know why, I couldn't think what she meant, or whom she was speaking to. When I came to, the blood jerked into my face because the sight of her sickened me; which struck me afterwards as rather absurd.

I am completely at ease strolling through the shadowy crowd to my car, I am absorbed into them. It doesn't matter that, for all I know, this is an illusion. The fact remains that fear has left me. I wonder if this change in me would have happened had Victor and I merely lived under one roof for convenience's sake and not because we are lovers. Intellectually I do not exist, nevertheless I start building a theory that without sex there can be no communication of any value whatsoever, I rule out all shadings in between. The inevitable next step is complete understanding among all men of all races. Some kind of universal love, for which there is lots of room. Giving them the vote won't help at all, what we must do is take them to bed.

I hurry on, longing to talk to Victor about it, he is so practical. And we are lovers again, in spite of all. If a blow on the back of the head comes at this very minute, at least I'll die a different person to the one I was a year ago and think of all the superb screwing there's been along the way.

It wasn't one of the things that Victor was conscious of but it went on tapping naggingly at the back of my mind. We were constantly being invited to the Stanfords – what could we do for them in return? Neither of them played tennis and I hadn't the nerve to give a dinner party. Six would be the minimum, and who would we collect as the other couple, and could I really manage to carry off a three-course meal in the unfussed way they were used to? As far as they were aware, of course, Victor lived in the township as the law demanded. More than likely, a part of Dick would have rejoiced to think of Victor and me extending our friendship into an arrangement by which we shared a house together. The law was the law, however, and no matter that the savagery of it made one's blood boil, while it existed it must be obeyed.

Victor was put on the late night programme, so I took them to a restaurant and the movies. No one ever asked them to the movies, couldn't we make it something special? Margaret said. Oh not one of those widescreen barns where nine times out of ten it turned out to be chariot races with Charlton Heston. Something, well, something you could get your teeth into, oh you choose, she said.

Scampi and duckling and a bottle of rosé put us in a lively mood and we hurried out of the candlelit restaurant to get to the movie in time for the credits. Once again they had revived *Le Blé en Herbe*, it was playing at the only art house in town. 'I've been dying to come here and Dick's been looking forward to this evening all week,' Margaret whispered as we went inside.

It was my first movie in six months, I found the people all around us disconcerting. I reacted to them with Victor in mind and I loathed them. Dick and Margaret were watching the screen like everyone else while I gnawed at a thumbnail. Salty little threads of blood tripped down my throat. At last I could hold out no longer against Feuillere's voice. I forgot my thumb. The boy was stiff as an actor instead of infusing this quality into the character he was playing, every scene belonged to Feuillere. Nothing that happened to the characters moved me in the least, Feuillere's performance blotted out everything else.

'Dick hated it. He's a moron,' Margaret said out loud in the foyer.

This astonished me, I wondered if Margaret were joking.

'Unhealthy,' said Dick

'Rubbish,' Margaret said.

'What do you mean by unhealthy?' she added.

'It's an unhealthy theme. Always did think there was something a bit messy about Colette.'

'You haven't answered my question. Do you know yourself what you mean by unhealthy? It doesn't sound like it.'

One or two faces in the crowd turned to examine Margaret. She said to Dick, 'Anyone would think you were a snivelling Wesleyan.'

Dick gave us both a tight little smile. 'Sorry, Ray, it's only an opinion.'

'One that needn't bother us another second.'

Margaret was angry, yet one couldn't be sure on whose account. Surely something more to it than simply a spoilt evening. Somehow I felt she was retracing old ground, often fought over with Dick before.

'Anyway who's for coffee?' I said.

Margaret decided for both of them. 'Love some.'

Up and down the street other cinemas were closing their doors. Women in furs, as though it were opening night at the opera, were stepping into cars. Four lanes of headlights swished down the street in front of our toes.

We made for a coffee bar with a rubber vine smearing its window.

'Ray, we really must join a film society. Let's you and I join together. I'll send them a cheque tomorrow.'

'There are only two in town and they've both got waiting lists.'

'No reason to give up so easily. We'll put our names down and hope for a plague. Dick'll pray too. His prayers are probably worth more than ours.'

Dick went on smiling as he lit his pipe. He had had his say and there was nothing fiery about his point of view and, try though she might, Margaret would never rouse him, failure being her daily bread.

I flared up when Theo told us he had nearly been sacked for taking on translation work from one of the oil companies.

'But it isn't a laughing matter. Theo, how can you laugh about it?'

'It all ended happily. I like my job and I'm still in it.'

'But it's the principle. How can you just sit back and take it and let them get away with it?'

'Ag, well,' he said, 'I knew the rule, we all do. No freelance work unless the fee is arranged beforehand with our boss and payment made to the SABC, not to us direct. And so the cheque comes from the SABC. Eventually,' he said.

'But they can't do it that way, it's immoral,' I said.

Victor rolled himself over on the lawn and faced us. An hour in the sun made his speech come slowly. 'Keep your hair on, there's nothing you can do about it.'

I said to them both, 'You know why they have this filthy arrangement? Because they pay you the bare bloody minimum and they know it. And they also know that, if you can get more for translating a couple of thousand words into Zulu for some oil company's house journal than they pay you in a whole week, they won't have an announcer left on their books.'

Victor sighed. 'Yes, we know this too.'

'And so. Why don't you do something about it?'

'Do what?' said Theo.

'Break the news to the chairman of just *one* of these American oil companies. What a stink he'd create once he knew his lousy PR department was actually playing ball with the SABC.'

Victor's criss-crossed fingers kept the sun out of his eyes. Whenever he needed his sunglasses they were nowhere to be found for some reason. 'So tell me,' he said, 'do you reckon the oil companies and the soap companies and the business machine companies would hire the lot of us once the SABC had fired us? They want their two thousand words of Zulu a month, that's all they want. Meanwhile Theo's got ten children.'

Bugger the principle. You've got to get down to the bare bones, you keep on forgetting this. For bare bones, read rotten facts.

'Ten,' said Theo, laughing softly. 'Time we had another one!'

In the end it always came back to the same thing, the brick wall. 'So you took a risk and you were found out and they didn't sack you. They warned you instead. For the first and last time. And that's why you were laughing so much.'

'Simple, hey?'

'Yes, isn't it. So simple it makes you sick.'

Theo grinned. '*You* maybe. I can't afford that sort of luxury.'

'I'll make coffee.' I jumped up, the garden see-sawed, dizzy green on all sides.

'Then we better be on our way,' I reminded Victor.

I said to Theo, 'We're going to see Victor's daughter, she's expecting him.'

I plugged in the kettle, I was alone with my thoughts. My only thought is to set fire to the world as I see it. I jumbled biscuits and custard slices on to one plate. Then I started again, I arranged everything neatly on two plates. Theo was paying us a state visit. For months he had been dropping hints until one day Victor said to me, I guess we'd better. But naturally. What's the point of us two sitting around making a private feast of our own happiness? In an idealised way Theo was in love with our happiness.

'Balls,' I said, 'there're lots more in the kitchen.'

Theo bit into his third custard slice.

How like an advertisement he looks with the yellow mush iridescent against his black cheeks.

When he had finished his coffee we led him down the garden to the sanitary lane.

'All our favourite guests leave this way,' I laughed.

He stopped again, he couldn't bear to tear himself away. 'Man, but it's nice here. You two have it lekker, hey!'

'You must come again. Come any time, Theo,' I said.

'When people start talking about folks who are in the pound seats I tell them they don't know what a pound seat looks like till they've seen you two.'

I caught Victor's eye. I said to Theo, 'Well, as long as you don't broadcast it to your forty million fans. You never know who might be listening in.'

He merely winked, then he was off down the lane.

I said to Victor, 'I like Theo but he talks about us to the wrong people.'

Victor shrugged. He was in one of those moods when nothing could alarm him, he would not lightly give up the sense of lethargy that so delighted him once he had allowed it to take over.

I said, 'We can wash up when we get back.'

He grabbed my hand. This startled me a little, he was normally so reserved outside bed. 'I like you best when you lose your temper,' he said. Many of the shrubs were in flower, fine fairy grass shifted soundlessly in the breeze under the deodar tree. We went up the garden into the house to change our clothes.

We stacked our parcels in the car and drove off. Victor was bringing clothes and school books. After much thought I had decided that necessities reeked of charity and who was I to the child anyway? For her birthday Victor had given her a record player. She liked groups, so I chose two records, one of them was the Stones pulling together beautifully.

'Right at the hospital, then straight on,' Victor said.

We would take a short cut through the western suburbs and link up with the Krugersdorp road at Honeydew. The child lived with her mother's aunt on a farm outside Krugersdorp, the farmer turned a blind eye to it all. I had no intention that the child and I should grow to love one another, it was simply that she was Victor's child and so it was right for us that I should know her.

The suburbs dribbled away and there were smallholdings next to the road. After the spring rains the earth glowed in between the peach trees. In the ramshackle little fruit stalls at the gate of each smallholding trays of apricots caught the light as children tilted them this way and that so that motorists could see them at their best and I thought, we haven't any fruit in the house, I must get a tray on our way home.

Every now and then cars whooshed past us on their way to Rustenburg or the game park. I said to Victor, 'It's lucky we're queer, isn't it?'

'What?'

'I mean no one bothers to look twice at us. I'm obviously a commercial traveller and you're my assistant so I don't have to carry heavy samples in and out of stores. Imagine how difficult life would be if I was a woman.'

'You have damn strange ideas sometimes, I'm telling you.'

We rambled on concocting one impossible situation after the other and making jokes about the general public in the way that people do because the reality has not happened. Victor's inventiveness soared far beyond mine. He astonished me and I roared with laughter. He could be flippant, like anyone else, but this wasn't really the true side of him, his wit was serious as a rule.

'Brakes. Left here,' he cried.

'Are we there already?'

'A couple of miles. The worst road in Africa. Can't get through when it rains.'

Even in low gear our heads smacked the roof every few yards. 'Those trees. That must be a river over there,' I said.

'Yes,' he said.

'Stop here,' he said, 'if you want shade for the car.'

One of those settlements you see on farms all over the country suddenly appeared next to the track. Clustered together three or four houses – I was going to say huts, but they were slightly bigger than huts and a different shape. Flat rusted iron roofs, walls made of packed mud and dung. Two bluegum trees behind and shiny beaten brown earth in front. A hen wandering dazedly into the veld that flowed in a single plane to the river. Presumably the farmer owned thousands of morgen, anyhow his house was out of sight somewhere.

Victor dropped down to hold his daughter, it wasn't a kiss as we understand it. Over his shoulder she peered at me almost flirtatiously.

They spoke in Sotho, her mother's family's language. Victor introduced me in English and ordered her to speak it too. She breathed a few words, then looked down. Her name was Audrey, somehow it was a name chosen for her in an idle moment. Victor kept his hand on the back of her neck while he smiled at me.

When the aunt came outside we switched to Afrikaans and we all laughed unsteadily, watching each other at the same time. The aunt was ablaze in a red crimplene dress and shoes with heels and a lovely satin doek round her head. I realised Victor had warned them I was coming. We brought out the parcels and Audrey returned straight away to the records once everything else was opened.

'She's her mother's daughter, what did I tell you,' Victor

said to the aunt, who pulled a face.

Dining room chairs, only in this case they were used for all purposes, were placed in a row at the front door. There was no suggestion that we should go inside the house. Neighbours from the other houses parted the long grass and inspected us, but before long they lost interest and I only heard their strangely pitched voices as though from far away.

Victor and Audrey chattered away together, he seemed to be teasing her about her school report. But all she did was to swing her legs sexily from side to side.

The aunt said to me, 'You are living in Johannesburg too?'

And so it went on. Her face was like a berry that has been creased into middle age by the pressure of delicate fingers, a subtly proportioned face. Her faintly bossy manner filled me with relief, I had dreaded a formality rooted in subservience.

Over the years her husband had risen to be the farmer's boss boy. Quite clearly she enjoyed his position.

'My husband he is fifty this year, myself forty-seven, we have no creditors,' she said.

Audrey giggled at her father whenever she was at a loss for words or felt my eyes turned towards her. My first sight of her amounted to nothing more than confirmation of what I had already accepted long ago. Out of Victor's sperm had sprung an oval face with scooped nostrils and greenish shadows overlaid on the dark skin beneath the eyes.

And what strain of your mother will come out in you? Her mother, who shopped for jewellery on Fifth Avenue and sang better than ever in support of Black Power at concerts in Caracas. In *Vogue* they had said of her, 'the most elegant shoulders in the world'.

The aunt had cooked a chicken stew and mounds of pumpkin that took on a sheen in the open air. Afterwards I left the three of them to talk freely among themselves and found a path through streaming grass down to the river. When I was well on my way there I heard Victor's voice calling.

'Don't get lost, hey.'

Standing up he almost reached the roof of the house. In his voice one could detect the anxiety of someone who would rather have been elsewhere. I thought, but it's only because you don't see enough of your child. You and she would grow into each other again if the two of you lived together, as you should, but can't.

I waved and went on my way.

Syrupy brown water spread into pools among rocks and the trunks of dead trees. I lay on my stomach on the riverbank playing with stones the colour of milky tomato soup. Fluttery little sounds went on recurring in the silence. I longed to get home again, yet a surface sense of ease kept me where I was. One was forever on edge, I assumed this must be a state of mind that went hand in hand with the circumstances. I visualised the two of us packing a suitcase and running off together that very night. In the next breath, temptation – to go on as we were, perhaps never being found out. Oh for Luxembourg. Andorra. I smiled at the lovely stones as though, having grown warm in my hand, they understood. Unlike me. I don't understand anything.

Nevertheless Victor and I were at peace again. From hatred (his) to hectic immediate lovemaking to peace again. The Stanfords' party was shunted off into that area inhabited by bad dreams that possibly never even occurred in the first place. As for that call to arms, well, it led astoundingly to goodwill on earth in the shape of early morning coffee in bed, a habit we had never got out of. That night, I think, each of us made a promise to himself, to persist in challenging the other till blood foamed on the kitchen floor. Apparently the next morning the challenge shrivelled and died. Or, if not quite that, at least kept itself well down, concealed inside tissues of which even we ourselves were unaware.

And then that claim that I wouldn't look twice at a black man in England. How do you know what your reaction will be in another country that you have never been to? All you know about yourself is the sort of person you are in your own country. Born blind, ordered to grow up blind, but not able to.

'Why did you run away from us?'

He was on top of the bank against the sky.

'Okay, I'm coming,' I said.

I threw away the stones and we walked back to the house and Audrey lifted a record from her record player and slid it into its sleeve.

'She needs new batteries, I forgot to get them,' Victor said.

'There's a shop near the office. I can post them on Monday. Is there a post office around here where she can collect them?'

Victor said, 'You see how everyone spoils you. Now you get down to your schoolwork and spoil me for a change.'

Audrey thought this very funny. She held on to Victor's waist, laughing into his jacket. The aunt came forward to take her hand, seeing that we were about to leave. I felt sad for Audrey and how lucky I was.

I looked across at the aunt, my thoughts were: does she miss her father?

One could see that the aunt was very fond of Audrey. But all the same my own happiness seemed to make Audrey's circumstances sadder still.

We drove away with Victor whistling to carry him over the first minute or two.

'You were nice to her. Thanks,' he said.

'I liked her. Now she has lots of new presents to keep her spirits up.'

'Poor old Audrey.' Then he added, 'I'm all right, I have you, hey.'

I swung left on to the main road. Only an hour and we would be in the city again, the curtains drawn. It would always astonish me that we so seldom got out of our depths.

Leave it to me, Frankie said. He fixed everything. He loved being at the helm.

A week in Beira. Victor and I were terribly excited. Neither of us had ever been outside our own country before.

First, Lourenço Marques. How shrewd the government had become. In its early days in power the answer to all requests that were ever so slightly adventurous was no no no and don't ask again. Slowly they were discovering how to make capital out of saying yes. After many months the show was about to close in Johannesburg. Word of mouth had carried its reputation all over Southern Africa and an invitation came in from a Portuguese arts council to take it to Lourenço Marques. The government agreed to issue temporary passports, for Mozambique only, almost before we had recovered from our sense of daring in having applied for them. Cultural links between embattled countries were second only to military ones, the spokesman said. And ja, an excellent idea to send along a State radio announcer who could report back on the good work being done by 'our Bantu artistes on foreign soil'.

Being more realistic about these things, the Portuguese were less pompous and gave us a marvellous time. Once the show had opened we left for Beira.

Frankie said, 'The days of tea dances in Lourenço Marques ended the minute some stooped loud-mouth leaked it to the Afrikaners that the escudo had been devalued. Ever since, the main praia has looked like the landing of Jan van Riebeeck.'

We flew above the deserted Mozambique coastline, cashew nut trees and jungle on the left. Horseshoes of off-white sand and greenish sea on the right. We were all delighted to be on our way and Frankie ordered nips of vinho espumoso to confirm the holiday spirit. Behind the port of Beira lies the Pungwe swamp and the raffish airport is bounded in shadow on all sides by forests strangled with vines. For the second time in a week Victor went through passport control and no one so much as gave him a once-over look and he and I smiled quickly at one another. My stomach muscles need no longer be kept in a tight sore ball on his behalf.

Our hired car had been parked in the shade of a mango tree and a porter soon filled up the boot with our cases.

We sailed towards the town and all the windows were open. I stuck my head out to catch that first whiff of the sea but we were not close enough yet. Yellow and pink and lilac houses unlike anything you came across in Johannesburg. No one went in for lawns here. Blazing red hibiscus bushes and mauve potato flower obviously thriving in putty coloured sand. Pools of rainwater on the sand were shrinking as you looked at them. Still no sea smell, but I picked up the custardy scent of oleanders overlapping the petrol fumes.

'Next one to the left, isn't it, precious?'

The house Frankie had taken for us belonged to the friend of a friend of a travel agent. We can just be ourselves and I can't think of nicer people to be, he had sung to me over the phone in Johannesburg.

The beach started at the bottom of the garden. I love harbour towns in vast bays outside of which, miles away, the ocean breakers crash out of sight and unheard. In the bay frilly little waves plopped on to the sand one after the other at a frantic speed. Beyond them the flat shallow sea went on and on to a blurred horizon.

Victor and I hurried up to the house where Frankie was inspecting rooms and talking about fresh vegetables. A Portuguese maid with a neat moustache but strangely hairless legs tagged along behind him. He leaned against a passage wall tapping his temple. Victor and I were given a front room on to the sea.

In the morning the sun rose swiftly on the sea horizon. Victor slept. I pulled on my trunks and ran outside where low slanted sunlight on the palm leaves cast a pattern of stripes all over the garden. A few steps and I was strutting about on the beach. The cool crusty sand crumbled away between my toes. I ran straight into the sea and swam around for a while and flushed water into my armpits. I picked up a rod of whitened bamboo and took it with me as a companion along the beach. By the time I reached the beach bar the seawater on my skin had evaporated, I felt clean right through to my bones.

'Are you open yet?' I asked.

'Twenty-one, twenty-two …'

A tiny hunchbacked man with banks of eyelashes looked up from a box of empties, above him the sun had just reached the raffia awning.

'Always for the customer we are open.'

'Cerveja, por favor.'

'Grande?'

'Sure – si.'

We smiled at the same instant, the first smile of the day, at least for me.

'Is it iced?'

'Gelada,' he said slowly so that I would get it right.

'Gelada.'

'Not bad,' he said.

Behind the beach bar rose a big white hotel at the end of an avenue of palms.

I bought cigarettes too, they tasted of nutmeg and were not nearly strong enough. But the beer was straight from heaven. Foreign beer. I dragged a metal chair across the pitted concrete floor into the sunlight and closed my eyes. Cling-clink-cling-clink went on behind me. Ninety-four, ninety-five. Cheers, they drank all day here. I dozed on and off. Selfishly I treasured the happiness I felt on my own. I looked forward to Victor's arrival, we would be happy all day, but the happiness would be of a different sort. Let me die now, after this it can only be downhill.

The sun in my eyes woke me, not voices. The feathery light around the sun had disappeared, and all the faint pearly wisps in the sky too. The sun shone in a hard blue sky like you might see anywhere. The saltiness of beer leaked from my teeth and I looked down at my watch, it was only eight o'clock.

When I turned sideways this man leaned forward in his chair as though he had been preparing himself for this for a long time.

Just my luck, a loner who is also a talker. My disappointment grew as I realised I would not be alone again all day.

'So it is you,' he said, and I saw he was only in his twenties though a fold of fat rested on the belt of his trunks.

He bounded across and shook my hand.

'Hello,' I said. Who *is* it? I recalled the face, but couldn't place it.

'I thought it was you,' he said.

'Nice to see you,' I said.

'You too.'

We fell silent, inspecting each other with little jerks of the head, occasionally swerving away to glance at nothing in particular.

'Small world!' he giggled. This was out of character.

Why're you so nervous? I should have asked him.

O'Connell. Of course. Head boy. Or first prefect? No, head boy, I think.

Followed by a small rush of confidence in my capacity to at least carry off this meeting without fading away altogether. Nevertheless I wished he would go away.

'Had a swim yet? Water's great.'

'My wife's still hogging it.'

Your wife. Naturally. I smiled at him, then stood up.

We trudged down to the water, he brought a towel with him.

'Still wear your hair on the long side, I see.'

'Have to. To cover up my mastoid scars.'

He chuckled after a pause of a few seconds. 'I farm tobacco,' he said, 'at Sinoia.'

'Where else can one farm it?'

He looked nonplussed, which I had not intended.

We reached the water. Purposely I cut past him and did a businesslike racing dive into the shallows and swam on for fifty yards or so. We kept ourselves a certain distance apart but we happened to come out of the water at the same time.

With his face inside his rapidly jerked about towel he said, 'We made a mistake coming to this place. Bloody awful food.'

'We're here forever. On the clear understanding that the prawns don't give out.'

'We?'

'How about a beer?' I said.

'Has he got Rhodesian beer – Stag?'

'Should he?'

The role of head boy is his crowning glory. But on the way up, in my first year at the school, he is a mere chapel prefect, along with twenty others. One in the middle of each alternate pew. Sing, he hisses. For the last time, *sing*. But for some reason or other you don't. And so a fist charges into the small of your back. My son's kidneys are there, a mother writes to Father Superior. Dear Mrs Dougherty, in my twenty-eight years in Jesuit colleges, the intestines of all boys being positioned, taking into account even the most eccentric variations, identically, not the slightest evidence of damage to … And on Fridays in Lent meditation on the playing fields to prepare us for Stations of the Cross at three o'clock. Calvary time. The captain of a team recommends meditation in pairs, behind the cricket nets. His randiness opens a new world. Dexterity, however, is something he will master later on, and anyhow emotionalism still bogs me down. So we get no further than an exchange of vows (always the same one) and breathy kisses. I adore his mouth and the smell of creosote with which they coat the cricket nets to make them last longer. Blazing behind me, my shirt tail provides all the wrong evidence when I take my place in chapel.

> Stabat mater dolorosa
> Juxta crucem lacrymosa
> Dum pendebat Filius.

O'Connell's fist, wham. I *am* singing, I say. Then try singing with your shirt in, he says. Our eyes meet. His are furious. But why? It can't be merely because I'm insulting the Lord. Perhaps he knows. He's jealous, I think. Maybe he doesn't even know he's jealous. Throughout the next verse I can hardly keep down my laughter.

> Sancta Mater istud agas
> Crucifixi fige plagas
> Cordi meo valide.

Leaving the chapel I see him watching me, eyes cold and sulky now. From him I learn of this particular power which, apparently, I possess. But what it's all about and how one turns it to good effect I haven't the least idea yet.

'Nothing to touch Stag,' he said.

'Why did you bother to leave home?' and, behind him, I saw Victor and Geoff coming towards us over the beach.

'Do you know any places where you can go at night?' he said. 'This hotel's dead.'

'There's the Oceanario. We ate there last night. You choose your fish out of a tank.'

'My wife doesn't eat fish.'

'Afterwards we went to that bar down by the port. They don't believe in closing hours in this town.'

'It's got atmosphere, has it?'

'Something like that.'

His face lit up. 'We might drop in one night. Just for a look-see.'

'Expect the worse,' I laughed.

'I think my wife would have preferred it down in South Africa. Say, Durban. Even Margate.'

'Next year they'll still be there. Well, here's Victor and Geoff.'

Now what? I thought.

The thing to do is to keep the action moving. An audience doesn't really want to think, it only thinks it does.

'Victor Butele, Geoff Grant. Henry O'Connell.'

Hands darted here and there. Murmurs followed.

'Henry was head of school once,' I said.

'Really?' said Geoff.

Henry looked from one to the other of us, giving Victor the quickest look of all of course. I wondered whether he would come out of his daze tomorrow or next week.

I had made up my mind to let Henry sort out appearances in whatever way he could, or must. No softening the blow. No gilt-edged reference to the show in which all we South Africans with our many coloured skins were working side by side in a common cause.

'You've missed the best swim of the day. Not to mention the best beer,' I said.

'After drinking the bar dry last night, you mean you've started again?' Victor said.

'You can't call beer a proper start,' I said.

Henry began bouncing distractedly from one foot to the other. Then he stared down at the sand.

'Anyway I'm getting in,' Geoff said.

Victor looked magnificent in his tartan boxer trunks. He appeared to be quite unaware of this.

'Where's Frankie?' I said.

Then a girl in a powder-blue beach robe slipped out of the avenue of palms on to the beach. Already the hotel had a glary look facing the sun.

The girl approached with her head down. But she knew there was no way of getting away from us.

'Frankie's cutting up fruit with the maid,' Geoff said.

'Ah Jeanette,' Henry said.

Such relief, yet apprehension. He managed to produce a nervous smile.

'You can't possibly remember all our names,' I said.

'Jeanette. My wife.'

'Victor Butele and Geoff Grant. Geoff's on the left,' I said.

Henry pulled out his trump card without waiting another second. 'The reason is, Ray and I were at school together.'

'Oh.' The girl seemed more startled than convinced. She

was spiky and pale with a thread of a throat. Her very light blue eyes turned to Henry and, with that, appeared not to move again.

Henry said, 'Did I wake you, Jeanie? I tried not to.'

She shook her head. The sun worried her, she fidgeted in her beach bag till she brought out a pair of tinted glasses.

Suddenly she broke out with, 'I haven't seen you in the hotel. You must have arrived last night.'

Geoff told her about our house.

'How lovely,' she murmured.

She never once focused on Victor, so far as I could make out.

'The water pressure's up the pole here, you should try our shower,' Henry said.

Frankie waved.

'Here's the rest of the family,' Geoff said.

Henry and his wife simply held hands.

'I've been in pawpaw up to my elbows,' Frankie called.

Everyone moved aside and there we were, in a ring on the sand. And more names. Years ago the man in the bar was counting bottles.

'Yes, it's a lousy hotel and one's memories of a holiday are more important than the holiday itself,' Frankie said.

'Yesterday the air conditioning packed up,' Henry said.

'The next time it happens thank your pet star you're not at the St Regis. After a summer in Manhattan this burg reminds one of mid-winter in Omsk.'

'Are there sharks in this sea?' someone said.

'You've got to be careful when the water's muddy,' Henry said.

'Henry, it's bad luck,' his wife said, 'even to mention them.'

Geoff's nose was twice as red as it was ten minutes ago and tomorrow it would peel. A long way off beyond the beach bar figures like sticks pranced on the sand.

Frankie said, 'One mad dip, then home to breakfast.'

'For the last time and who knows if we will ever see it again,' Frankie said, suddenly downcast.

'We'll all come back one day,' I said.

Yet I knew this would not be so. On the beach last night, while the sun went down behind crumbly clouds, Victor and I had decided. The thought of this, alone, made me so excited my stomach croaked and I could hardly get a sensible word out. I was terribly nervous too, but it wasn't like the old nervousness. Our high hopes had put an end to that sort. When we go, Victor had said, we mustn't slip away like we're ashamed of anything or scared. We must go properly, like other people do. Leave it to me, I had said.

'Yes, it's a good bar,' Geoff said. 'Frankie found it of course.'

On our last night, in our dark suits like businessmen, we turned up there as a matter of course. Not even Henry could ruin it, though he tried hard enough, in his silly way.

In the hot light of the bar, the regulars bellowed at one another close to the counter. For the last drink of the night, perhaps, we might go inside. But it was on the pavement that everything happened and we were all panting for cool air. We sat round a table with fluted legs. Curly iron pillars fanned out into latticework higher up in the darkness of the roof. Any minute, Blanche might drift into view and *Streetcar* would begin. The square, however, was another world altogether. Humpy cobbles that glinted fleetingly under lamps and a border of plump trimmed trees and a fountain in the middle. Given daylight, Cézanne. But we only ever came here at night. Sailors rolled into the square from the harbour, which was next door. When the cognac began to work you could reach out and touch the sides of ships.

'Your school prefect has come to spy on you,' Geoff said.

'Don't encourage him,' Frankie hissed, keeping his teeth together while he smiled vaguely at Henry and his wife.

They found a table. I nodded to them over my shoulder, the others picked up their glasses and went on drinking.

'They'd give anything to join us,' I said.

'This is no time for charity. Drink up, children,' Frankie said.

'Your friend is one of those people who always remembers to keep his jacket buttoned up on foreign soil,' Victor said.

'You travel a lot, do you?'

This was the nearest we dared come to airing our secret in public.

Under cover of a fresh round of drinks arriving at the table he whispered into my ear, 'I can't get it out of my mind, and you?'

'Can't sleep, don't want to.'

'Wish we could wake up tomorrow in, where, Malaga?'

'Think of it. A new life. Not a minute too soon either.'

'You two. Stop it,' Frankie said.

So we took our drinks, the last two on the table. Rugged brandy with a sticky underlining. Hey, God, be a sport, let Victor and me live forever.

Victor turned to Geoff, I watched their mouths opening and closing. Is it my imagination, does he look younger already? More sure of himself? He carries his head up high. A sense of freedom or something? He won't have to scuttle about on the face of the earth ever again. He will be the equal of everyone, only better than most. For him it'll be like growing up all over again, except that the direction of growth will be his own choice, not one foisted on him by the latest amendment to the last Amendment Act.

Once again the Portuguese boys flew past us, then slowly returned. A boy leaned back against the pillar, he was in no hurry. His young-old eyes kept watch on each of us in turn. From now on he ignored his friends. They plodded up and down arguing about where to search next.

Fresh glasses floated on to the table. The fat oval cognac bottle splashed down into the glasses.

'Yes, there's plenty of room,' I heard Victor say.

The sailors dropped to their haunches next to Frankie. Their hair was as wild as straw and their eyes blue. Frankie ordered beers for them, he loved company.

Holland-Afrika-lijn, they told us.

Frankie's outlines had softened already, he melted in the blast generated in his imagination by the presence of the sailors. And so it was that one caught a faint flicker of the early Frankie, in the days when none of us knew him. From his secure perch now he inspected the same old material, the difference being that today he treated jokingly what once upon a time was a serious matter.

'You know, I'm a bit drunk,' I told Victor.

He burst out laughing. I laughed as well, it was ridiculous, we couldn't stop. Both inside the bar and on the pavement noise and lights and noise and lights and nothing else while everyone was making of it the night of his life.

In Frankie's hand lay a silver medallion. The medallion was still attached to a cord that hung from the sailor's neck. The sailor and Frankie examined the medallion with dazed faces.

A scream rose up, then up again, in a street off the square. Frankie clapped his hands. 'Someone's being raped. It's not me and I'm furious.'

It was Henry beside me and his breath smelled unhealthy and he spoke right into my ear. He said something on these lines: 'This is a disgrace by any standards.'

I backed away in order to bring him into focus. Such sullen eyes burning me up from a foot away.

I said, 'What? What did you say?'

'You are creating a bad impression here,' he said.

I said, 'I'm drunk. But even when I'm not drunk I create what I like.'

'So you mix with anybody now. Kaffirs, anybody. Don't you obey any rules any more?'

'I know why you look different. You're pissed too.'

'The whole damn lot of you have got no sense of res-ponsibility, do you understand?'

I reached out to find Victor. 'Listen to this fool,' I said to him.

'I heard him. Go screw yourself,' Victor said to Henry.

'Enough of that,' Frankie called across the table.

'I'm talking to Ray,' Henry said.

'Permission granted. As long as you stick to party manners,' Frankie said.

The sailors stood up and took their hands out of their pockets and faced Henry as though this were the most natural thing in the world to do.

'People like you should stay in your own country,' Henry said to us.

'Is this your country? Is that why you're being so possessive?' Geoff enquired.

'You wouldn't have the guts to behave like this in your own country,' Henry said.

Frankie pointed to Henry. 'A tobacco farmer with a sense of style. How refreshing. Pull up a chair, shitface, and somebody bring on the deadly nightshade.'

Hot bitter streaks of liquid with lumps were hitting the top of my throat and I was pushing them down again and again.

I said to Henry, 'I'm going to fuck you up.' I stood up. I just managed it. I said, 'Don't ask me why I'm doing this. Because you're too late. Doesn't matter any more. People like you don't matter to us any more. But purely as a gesture.' My hand curled itself into a fist without any special concentration on my part. I hit Henry on a cheekbone and I remember him shaking his head from side to side like they do in prize fight movies and I was delighted about this. Figures hurried in between us of course. So that was that, the fight was over.

I said the Victor, 'You know what, it's a mistake to mix beer and brandy.'

'Feeling all right?'

'I really am a bit drunk, I'm sorry. How's Henry?'

'You're tremendous when you lose your temper, I've told you this before.'

'From now on I'm going to stick to – '

Anyway I was still on my feet, or this was the impression I hoped to create. Victor's arm not only held me up but set me in motion. I picked out a whitish smudge, which must have been Henry's wife's face, a long way off, then nearer. The cobbles reared up like the Himalayas, but we must beat them because the car was the best place for me, Victor said.

'Christ, I'm sorry, I hate people to get drunk,' I said. 'You won't leave me, will you,' I added.

'You're doing well,' he said. 'Only another ten yards. Do you want to be sick?'

'Later. I don't know.'

I stretched out on the back seat and all the windows were open and I no longer minded having made a scene.

'That bastard, who does he think he is?' I said.

'He's not even a bastard, just a cunt. Are you all right now?'

'Thanks for everything,' I said.

'Some water,' he said, 'iced?'

'I'm off liquid of any sort.'

Victor was shaking with laughter close beside me, then he jumped out of the car and I saw his face in the window. 'Do you mind if I go back? Must see how this all ends.'

'Don't pick a fight with anybody and remember what they all say and tell me tomorrow.'

Down at the harbour a ship's hooter echoed and I thought, what a lovely sound. Will we go by air or sea? Air's faster, sea's cheaper. All our things. But when you work it out, what have we got? Nothing but our clothes luckily. And so by air. Which airline? What a lot to think about.

I sat up by the window when my stomach had stopped rocking and there they all were outside the bar in the half-light. Henry's wife clutching a pillar and arms circling the air and heads jerking this way and that and a fist shooting out but knocked aside before it could land and a finger pointing, then many fingers, and no soundtrack. Just another argument, how futile. But not to worry. Quite soon none of this would concern us any more. This lovely backwater of a seaport town on the east coast of Africa that half the world had never heard of and why should they.

3

'Now now, it's not like you to be sentimental,' Dick said.

'But it is,' I said.

We smiled at each other across his desk. When it came to silence, he could outlast me by years. At board meetings, so they said, he spoke very little. When he did, it was to push out encouragement to others to have their say. Right at the end he might dart in with a single comment that resolved everything. On the other hand, he might not. Observers were in two minds about what went on inside that beautifully carved head.

The head itself impressed me deeply.

'But you can't get away from it. The scholarship has never been given to an African. Why hasn't it?' I said.

'It is awarded on merit,' he said. He thought for a while. 'Promise as well,' he added.

'Does that mean Victor's too old? He's about thirty-five,' I said.

'Not in the least.' He set off on a small journey on his swivel chair, then returned to face his desk. 'And I like the idea. The winners in the past few years have been ... let me see. A pianist, a ballet dancer, a violinist – '

'A painter, if not two. I looked up the file.'

'Yes, that Feldman girl got it one year.' Dick scrawled something on a pad. 'The Organisation does like to feel that the people it chooses come into contact over there with influences that don't exist here. If their work doesn't benefit in some way, what are we doing it for?'

'There's tremendous scope in London for a broadcaster and it would make a nice change after all the cellists.'

Dick laughed. 'Don't worry, I'm on your side,' he said.

I pushed back my chair a fraction. Nothing about working

for the Organisation gave me more pleasure than knowing Dick's door was always open to me. This did not mean, however, that I could select my own ground with him. It was a case of following his lead, he couldn't conceive of it being otherwise, whether in fact he himself realised this or not. I respected him and I liked him and I was scared stiff of overstaying my welcome.

'I'll get London office to make some enquiries about study courses and who runs them and ... they're awfully helpful, there's nothing they don't know about. I'm glad you popped in,' he said. He smiled. 'Strictly between you and me of course, I can't see any reason why we shouldn't pull it off.'

Someone resigned so Victor's night shift was extended and whenever an opportunity came to go out at night I grabbed at it. I couldn't sit still on my own for five minutes, let alone a whole evening. We were both very strung up at this time, waiting to know if we could leave in the way we hoped to.

Johannesburg was so proud of its new civic theatre, but for me it was merely a place in which to spend a few hours in the company of others. The province's ballet troupe was dancing *Giselle*. Frankie flinched and closed his eyes. Nevertheless the applause at the end was enough to blow you inside out.

'I'll never believe it really happened,' Frankie said.

Geoff told him to shut up, that he was spoiling the pleasure of others.

'Masochists get beyond that stage,' Frankie said.

He threw his programme under his seat and stamped on it. We trailed slowly up the carpeted stairs among knees and elbows. Everything was gold and ginger and beige and the acoustics were terrible. They had cost a fortune. Twinkly stars in the ceiling and then, smack, the foyer. So much puce one fell silent.

We stood outside on the terrace drawing in fresh air.

'The Wilis shouldn't *thunder* into the shades,' Frankie said. 'It isn't proper.'

'Not all of them did,' Geoff said.

'You weren't listening.'

Geoff steered us down the steps to the car park. 'They're a young company. Give them time,' he said.

'Not a second more of mine. Now let's make a dash for home and tea on the rocks. You'll follow us?'

I told them I must get back before Victor came in.

'Just the merest sip?'

I thanked them for taking me and asked them to eat with us on Saturday.

He would phone me at the office, Frankie said.

'Drive safely,' said Geoff, who said this to everyone, but in a way that was never offhand.

Once I was inside my car my conscience moved in to attack. I felt I had let Victor down all over again. From all outside appearances I no longer minded going to places from which he was barred. The reason for my doing so seemed nothing but a feeble excuse when you really examined it. Staying power was absolutely crucial, yet what was happening to mine? Was I the sort of person who gives up on the last stretch and was only discovering this about himself tonight?

As though to make my conscience easier to live with, I leaped forward from traffic lights ahead of everyone else. I turned the car viciously into our road and roared into our garage and jumped out and ran towards the front door.

It was a still summer night with the wind high up and smooth clouds around the moon. The telephone was ringing.

The key had been slightly bent from the beginning, you had to slide it in at a subtle angle. Eventually it turned. The telephone stopped ringing.

Wrong number obviously.

I tossed my jacket on the bed, then went to find a hanger, then left it where it was. In the kitchen I poured myself a brandy and sucked at it while glancing down at a layout I had brought home from the office. Plenty of white and well placed. Not bad, I thought. Type's a bit light, Gill's a gutless face.

I wandered round smoking a cigarette. How limp and shabby everything looked. After having scaled down our original excitement at moving into the house we had decided to leave everything as it was more or less.

The phone rang and I was there within seconds.

'Hello.'

'Mr Starle?'

'Yes.'

Nothing for a moment, then 'This is Parkside police station.' Afrikaners speaking English, or what they believe to be English. That harsh way of dealing with words, like a chopper might. Traffic cops, railway porters, bus conductors, postmen. No wonder they hate us, lumping them all together at the bottom of the ladder. But aren't they happier there? my mother once said, not intending to raise a laugh.

He's not dead, that's one thing I'm certain of. I waited.

'You have a boy, a servant? Simon Dube?'

Simon Dube?

Make up your mind, yes or no.

'That's right,' I said.

'We have him here. Parkside police station.'

'What's he done?' I said.

'No pass.'

Is that worse than murder? I can't remember just for the moment.

'I'll come round now,' I said.

'He can speak to you. Hang on.'

Whispers – is that all? Or are they bending his bones next to the mouthpiece?

'Master?'

You conjure up all sorts of horrors in advance, but funnily enough never the one you are eventually faced with. Afterwards you can laugh over it together.

'Simon, what's the trouble?' I got out.

'They pick me up and my pass is not with me.'

How superb he is, the accent is flawless.

'Please, master?'

'Yes, Simon.'

'Please the master must bring money for the fine.'

'You're a damned nuisance, you boys. How much money do they want?'

'Plenty, master.'

'See you,' I said.

I got up from the floor where I had fallen. I went into the kitchen and finished the rest of my brandy and drank more from the bottle.

White masters always reek of brandy – or should it be whisky? – when they're called to the police station to pay their servants' fines at eleven-thirty at night.

The brandy brought the bones back into my knees, which was the important thing. Money. The money. Plenty, master. Bunch of crooks – how dare they? Don't *think*, I told myself. Lots of time for that tomorrow and next year and the rest of your life.

Victor sometimes pushed notes under his shirts and I found these and some silver and my own cash, which was in my pocket, leaky with sweat now, and more in a biscuit tin in the kitchen. Fifty-three rands plus the silver. Fifty-six, say.

Meanwhile the clouds had cruised away from the moon. What a perfect summer's night. I hate this summer's night and the house and the garden. The clouds were quite different to the fluffy clouds usually seen in the sky summer after summer. They looked manufactured, like sleek metal cylinders.

Each suburb has its own police station, often an oldish house (picked up cheap) with the sitting room converted into a charge office, bars plugged across the windows, and the Parkside police station was one of these. No sign of a lawn any more. A worn dusty space to park your car in and sad drab wattle trees against the moon. Though the evening peak hour had passed, half a dozen cars were still drawn up in the light of the stoep. Women in Jaguars smoked sulkily while their husbands shot inside to bail out the cook-boy, without whom the household would crumble away.

Men in houndstooth jackets and paisley scarves lounged about the charge office while black constables with dreamy eyes drifted this way and that. The white policemen were behind the counter filling in forms. I'm hopeless at identifying rank. All police uniforms look equally badly cut and on which sleeve do you find the stripes that tell all?

I gave my name when one of the policemen raised his head eventually. Take a seat, I was told.

'Servants' – alongside me on the bench – 'I thought this was the great compensation of living at the arse end of Africa.'

'My God, times have changed.'

'My wife's livid. Cook spends more time here than in the kitchen.'

'Wrecked our bridge. We were in the middle of a rubber. Third time it's happened.'

The hours passed, or was it not more than twenty minutes all told? Occasionally a man in houndstooth would glance at me. He saw the son of the house probably, or the daughter's fiancé, or the chairman's PA who watchdogs the house while the chairman is ski-ing at Klosters.

'My' policeman then entered. He summoned me over and I put out my cigarette out of force of habit. Their uniforms in South Africa are a grey-blue. It is not a particularly startling, or even distinctive, colour. Made up into some other kind of garment you wouldn't look at it twice. But even today when I see the same colour in a crowd that coldness in the stomach comes back again.

'Yes,' I said, 'with an "e" at the end.'

He wrote very slowly and the carbon kept on crimping. An original plus two copies, I noticed.

I signed my name at the bottom of the form while he watched me, I could feel it.

No mention of the fine yet. 'In here,' he said.

I followed him into a small room which was empty. The beautiful old moulded ceilings had been left intact.

'Your boy is one of those educated ones, hey?'

'He never struck me that way. He's just a boy, like any other.'

He let it pass, yet gave the impression of noting it in his mind. Did it come off my tongue too easily – not easily enough?

But – cheer up, he hasn't even got a mind.

'Your boy has no pass,' he said.

'I'm in the process of – ' Why do they always have this effect on you of even changing the way you put things? 'I'm going through the proper channels but it takes time,' I said.

'He is in your employ illegally.'

Such a babyish pink-and-white skin and your eyes aren't too bad either, you great big shit.

'A boy must have a pass to work in this area. The municipal area of Johannesburg,' he said.

'I'm expecting it to come through any day now.'

'Your boy can be sent back to his place of birth. He is committing an offence here. Also he is liable to a fine.'

The electric light bulb was behind his head, it was my face that took the brunt. 'How much?' I said.

He waited and I thought, this is a trap, they know everything.

'Fifty rands,' he said.

'I've got it here.'

He shrugged but soon afterwards he half smiled.

Now? Or am I rushing things?

He made no sign, so I pulled out my notes. I gave him four tens, a five and five ones and he glanced down at them in his pale meaty hand and folded them and put them inside his jacket into a pocket out of sight.

'Wait in the charge office,' he said.

The charge office was an easygoing place after the ambiguity of the back room. I sat in a corner feeling strangely elated. One of the paisley scarves returned from a room opposite the one I had been taken to and I wondered how much he'd been asked for and what happens to the forms in triplicate and one thing they certainly economise on in this place is receipt books.

And then Victor was brought in, his face bitter behind the smile, and the absurdity of it all no longer came through to me. In its place was sheer anger, which quickly swept on to become transformed into a craving for revenge. I managed to nod goodnight to the policeman, who stood behind the counter watching us till the end, and to walk outside ahead of Victor without offering him more than a grunt. The light of the stoep reached the car, and beyond, and Victor climbed into the back seat as though he had always done so and I drove off. At last we came to the road and after two blocks I said, 'There's a drink waiting for you and you must be dying of hunger.'

'A bottle or two of brandy and I'll be fine.'

'What happened?' I said.

'What do you mean, what happened? What do you think happened?'

'They picked you up – but where?'

'They pick up hundreds of us every night. What's so special about that?'

'I don't care about the others, I'm – '

'Sure you don't. Who does? Apart from the others themselves and the people in their lives.'

'I'm asking about you.'

I heard Victor sigh.

'Okay, forget it,' I said. 'We can talk tomorrow.'

'Why tomorrow? Can't you take it? I'm not entering into the spirit of the thing, and then there're your shaken up nerves to consider, right?'

'Okay, no more questions. I'm not interested.'

'What happened tonight isn't the end of the world. I got a lift to Oxford Road and started walking. A police van drew up at the corner of Cotswold and a cop asked me for my pass. My pass states that I work at the SABC and I live in Soweto township, extension R. A fat lot of good that pass does for me these days.'

He whistled limply, bored with the story he was telling. 'Listen, man, you know the plan we cooked up as well as I do and all I can say is I stuck to it. "Sorry, sir, my pass he isn't through yet." You paid the fine and I'm free. Free,' he repeated, chuckling to himself in the back seat.

'I took your money too to pay the fine,' I said.

'You mean I should congratulate myself?'

We got home in silence and crossed the garden to the front door.

'Will you have sandwiches or something hot? Both are easy,' I said.

'What if I ask for something difficult?'

I closed the door behind me and he walked away to the bedroom and I should have put my arms around him but I didn't. I told myself that for the moment he was beyond anything I could do for him, which was nonsense of course, and showed up both my cowardice and my arrogance.

I tipped ice into our drinks and switched on the stove and broke eggs into a bowl. Victor wandered in after a while and picked up his drink. He watched me making omelettes.

I said, 'Looks like the time has come for us to start thinking of moving on from this house to somewhere else, what do you think?'

'You asking me? It's up to you. You're the one who makes the decisions and carries them out. What the hell can I do?'

Nobody's irreplaceable, it's an accepted fact. I'm all right at my job but anyone could take it over at a day's notice. Bosses play around with you in the beginning. It amuses them to watch you paddling about in the shallows. You can't do any harm there. It's only later on that things get serious. Only those of us who manage to erect another storey on to early promise are selected for the heights. I'm not one of those. I have no second wind. Nor the ambition to build it up. I'll slip as I grow older, I've always suspected this. People here seem unaware of this. They should raise up a 'Te Deum' when I leave. The idiots, they won't of course. Instead, they'll feel let down, or at least that's what they'll say. Dick especially no doubt. But he really will feel it, I think. Dick alone, of all of them.

I kept to myself in the lunch hour so I could go over these thoughts undisturbed. Only after I had spoken to Dick about the scholarship for Victor did I see fully the position in which I had put myself. Should Victor win the scholarship I would have to resign so that we could leave together. Dick would then measure it all up and he would feel I had not only used him but betrayed him. What a mess I had made of it.

If only I'd talked it over with someone before rushing in while the blood still flapped in front of my brain. And all the time I'd thought, how shrewd you are. So balanced, so practical. Instead of a cloak and dagger escape via Swaziland or Mozambique I had considered the future. Victor's child, my parents. No question of cutting ourselves off from them forever. After all, we might want to return here one day and how much simpler everything is when you have a passport (and that comforting citizen status that goes with it) and can come and go with the assurance that there is nothing wrong with you, visibly, anyway. Victor's only chance of getting a passport was if he were awarded a scholarship or a bursary or were a member of some kind of delegation or were invited abroad in some official capacity – but what, for instance?

Oh stuff it, I'll think of some way of explaining it all to whoever will listen one day.

I jumped up and went back to checking Press kits for the chairman's meeting that afternoon. I had been moved from design to the press section as the second stage in my education as a public relations officer and once a year the chairman met the press and gave them cocktails and told them roughly one half of what they wanted to know about his company's operations. Everyone in the department became very tense and defensive as the day wore on and at last we all trooped downstairs to the boardroom.

I wore one of the ties Victor had brought home the day after he had been picked up by the police. They were gift-wrapped and I found the box on my pillow and my first thought was how he hated going into smart shops uptown. He couldn't carry it off like those Africans whose compulsion is to snap up the best clothes at the highest prices because, after all, what else can they own that tells the world that they've arrived? Change them if you don't like them, he said rather gruffly. I wouldn't dream of it, even if I didn't, I told him. That was a ridiculous attitude, he said. That was his opinion, not mine, I said. I put on all the ties, one on top of the other, violet and bottle green and gold among them, all of a type of heavy satin, by Pucci, I remember. I kept them on and he began to laugh and we were friends again, though that was all for the moment, we were friends. The fine had ruined us temporarily and we were living on macaroni and boerewors till the end of the month, so the beautiful ties swept away the air of austerity in the house.

I am a South African, said the chairman, who was hurrying back to Cap d'Ail in the morning, and I believe in the future of South Africa.

The press lazed in padded chairs beneath the damask curtains. The curtains were oysterish and double-lined. I glanced through the soundproof windows at the traffic trudging noiselessly up the street.

Record output for the seventh successive year, the chairman breathed. Record profits. But having disclosed this, and the press looked so bored, a note of warning. The press perked up. Labour, the chairman mouthed. Skilled labour. The country's Achilles' heel, in fact. Neither production nor profits could be maintained at current level, let alone a higher one, unless the government's labour policy was revised. African advancement was not only crucial but humane. Present protective legislation damaged all races. The ultimate victim? – the nation itself. I have been accused, am repeatedly accused, of pursuing job advancement of my African employees for the purpose of displacing white workers. Why do I wish to do this? My wicked master plan is interpreted in either one of two ways.

On the one side I am told my intention is to elevate Africans to higher jobs but to pay them less than whites in those same jobs, on the other side I am described as an irresponsible liberal determined to disrupt this country's traditional way of life no matter the cost.

The melancholy Hebraic eyes fixed themselves on the middle distance. Such eyes. When your eyes are spectacular and your nature secretive, how clever to blind the observer to everything but the spectacle of those eyes. Behind them the hiding place stays intact. I, we, of this Organisation will continue to condemn this law but, while it remains in force, we will carry on our operations in strict accordance with it. There is no other way. In the interests of our companies, our shareholders, our employees of all races, our country. I believe.

Alone in the house at night I listened to his voice on our radio and they wrote him postcards by the hundreds. Dear Victor Butele, we get a real kick out of you but why don't you play Hound Dog for us no more, don't let us down please yours faithfully. Dear Mr V Butele, your programmes are the best definitely and you could hear a pin drop in our lounge the time you are on the air, thanks for Hazel Xoma singing Click-Click any chance of hearing it again one of these fine days, you've really put that girl on the map, sincerely yours. Dear Mr Butele, that time you spoke from the city of Lourenço Marques came over as a big pleasure for us, tell us more about it can you if you have the time to spare, it is crazy and free there and a person can live a good life, yours in appreciation.

Luckily I had the sense to switch the band to another programme when the doorbell rang. Frankie and Geoff? Could be. Once before they had dropped in on their way back from dinner somewhere. But somehow I didn't expect it would be them and one did things out of sheer instinct more and more nowadays and sometimes this coincided with common sense.

The two men stood there under the carriage lamp.

A policeman who was new to me, but in the usual uniform, and a doughy faced man with a mere flick of a moustache in a sports jacket and fawn pants. What made this man stand out was the faint greenish light playing round his lips.

The sight of the two of them together tipped me off balance immediately.

'Afrikaans of Engels?' the detective said.

'English. You can speak either. It makes no difference.'

But they don't always like to be told this, it denies them the sense of superiority that goes hand in hand with their being obliged to speak your own language because of your ineptitude with theirs.

They pushed on in English as though they hadn't heard me. The policeman showed me a search warrant. I assumed a practised eye and looked down at it. So it was Central Square now, not our own little local Parkside round the corner.

'Over to you,' I said.

They were inside our house, their presence changed the house forever.

'Coffee? Or a drink?' I said.

They shook their heads simultaneously and looked around. 'We have received a report,' the detective said.

The 'A' programme news was announcing its headlines. Opening the new Elandslaagte Dam in the western Transvaal today, the Minister of Water Affairs said, Water is vital.

'Is it a bit loud? I'll turn it down,' I said.

'It is reported that Bantu people are seen on this property,' the detective said.

'My servant?'

'Do you mix socially with your servant?'

A collector's item if laugh lines were what you collected, but all I said was, 'No, why do you ask?'

'The report states that Bantu peoples have been playing tennis here and fraternising in your company.'

I smiled, making sure I did so neither provocatively nor patronisingly. 'I have African friends and they drop in from time to time.'

'By African – you mean Bantu?'

'Yes.' They themselves hate Bantu. Is that why it's been chosen as the new official word?

'Complaints have been made,' the detective said.

'I've had my friends here, there's no law against it,' I said. 'Not against a cup of tea.'

He looked me over without the faintest trace of expression on his acre of face. 'Correct. There is no law, up to a point,' he said, 'as yet.'

He said, 'How many occupants in this house?'

'I'm on my own here,' I said.

'Only one occupant – you?'

'I'm not married. Not yet,' I added.

Then the policeman joined in. 'You have a servant. Name of Simon Dube. We have a report,' he said.

'About his pass?'

But you mustn't try to set your own pace with interrogators. Their formula is their own and you must learn this.

'Show us his room.'

'What *was* his room. I sacked him,' I said.

For the first time a flicker of human frailty behind the iron mask. The policeman frowned at the detective. The policeman seemed put out for a moment.

'Where is the room?'

They followed on my heels down the passage to the kitchen which smelled of the frozen pizza pie I had hotted up for my supper.

Above us was a freakishly cold summer sky. Without warning snow had fallen a hundred miles south at Volksrust for the first time in November since the great drought years. Snow breaks drought. People still talked about it.

The big greasy key slithered in the keyhole, then we went inside.

The neatness of the room worried me. Did it remind one of a stage set, pieced together for an audience? I stood next to the door while they ferreted around with terrifying profession-alism.

'He said he'd come back next month for the rest of his clothes,' I told them.

They ignored this, the policeman said, 'Where is his place of birth?'

'Near Tzaneen somewhere.'

'He has returned there?'

'That's what he said. But you know these people. They say one thing. And then?' I shrugged, blowing out my lips.

Both the policeman and the detective turned round to examine my expression in relation to the remark I had made.

You used to be pretty good at playing stock characters, maybe you aren't any more, I was thinking.

They tossed a pair of shoes into a corner and yanked a suit from the cupboard.

I know the body inside that suit. Not that he wears it any more. It never fitted properly and he can't bear clothes that bulge and droop. That's why it's here, you maniacs. Why do I love this man who used to wear this suit? The hopelessness of our relationship – is this what attracts me?

I wanted to scream at these men, there is *nothing* hopeless about it. Just by your being here, that's enough to put words into my mouth. Don't think you can make me do it again.

'This Simon Dube,' the policeman went on. 'You say he is no longer in your employ?'

'He kept on saying he was going to get his pass fixed up but he never did so I paid him off. Another of those fines and I'd have been bankrupt. Who do you think I am, Rockefeller or someone?'

They stared back at me beneath the light bulb and I had confidence now and I knew I could beat them.

But bloody Christ don't let them stay all night. Another half hour at the most. Was their van parked in the street outside? Victor would see it, he'd have the sense to stay away.

'We will see the house,' the detective said.

Even in the undergrowth nothing moved. Moonlight strained through leaves on to the mouths of arum lilies in a hollow. The snowy air tore away all scents except that of the stocks against the wall, it wasn't like being in our garden at all.

The detective pressed on. 'So you keep this place clean on your own, you tell me.'

'Since the boy left it's never been cleaner. Ever heard of a thing called a Hoover?'

'But even so.'

'These kaffirs, they don't get through work like we do.'

'But you have them as friends, hey?'

'We're talking about servants, aren't we? My friends aren't servants.'

Our eyes met as we passed through the kitchen.

'Dis snaaks.' This is strange.

Failure was making them cross and they were letting it show. More than likely they would not permit me to witness this again.

The bedroom interested them more than any other room, needless to say. Do they inspect the sheets in the hope of finding little springy black hairs? I wonder if male body hair is different to female?

They opened drawers and, as I lit a cigarette, I frowned through the smoke in front of my face at the jar of cold cream beside the bed. It became the pivotal point of the room, I couldn't take my eyes off it. Some quite ordinary brand. Ponds probably. There it stayed, even though weeks might pass without our having need of it. Then I would reach out for it one night and scoop it up and spread it blindly in the dark. Its particular candy odour seemed to crowd the room and I began to blush, which made me want to laugh, all things considered. I turned aside, they might pick up a clue.

But impossible. Not a fragment of a spark in either of them, all they can do is carry out orders. Remember when tapping phones first came into fashion. You picked up your phone and on the end of the line it was like Guy Fawkes' night.

His clothes and mine overlapped in one wardrobe, one chest of drawers. Unless they went through them collar measurement by collar measurement ...

The detective's eyes kept on returning to the bed. The expression on his face became more and more agitated. When I glanced down at my cigarette I could feel him looking at me.

A lump of a man, yet a certain inappropriate delicacy showed up like a shadow in his movements.

When he flipped the cover from the bed he dragged out my pyjamas, which were green, I remember. Almost immediately he let them drop.

His actions mystified me. Probably they are meant to, I thought.

'Show us your books,' he burst out.

'Sure you won't have a drink?' I said.

I wondered how they could possibly store in their minds the hundreds of titles declared unfit for us by the *Government Gazette*. Perhaps their training was erected on the foundation of a dozen or so words that pointed the way. Revolution. Comrade. Rapture. Norman Mailer. Communist. *Chatterley*. Naked. Socialism. Clitoris.

Betti's *The Queen and the Rebels* turned out to be the only book that bothered them. Double threat, to say the least. Which queen? A British one? If so, monarchist propaganda. But which was the greater evil, a queen on her throne or revolutionaries cutting down her empire from under her? Reluctantly, it seemed, they stuffed the book back into its shelf.

Once more at the front door at last and they told me to sign something.

Am I free or not?

You can't just leave me without a word.

But how naive of me. This was their method. My nerves were no concern of theirs. Or rather, they were of course. Leave his nerves on hooks and see what that does to him.

Their van drove off almost inaudibly. I locked the door and

went to fetch the brandy and the next minute I was shaking all over and I slopped precious brandy on the kitchen table and it began leaking through cracks on to the floor before I could get my head down and suck up more than a few shreds of it. I drank it from the bottle and the shaking stopped for a while.

I must have been an odd sight trotting from room to room in an effort to keep calm so that I could think straight. A part of me longed to give in and cry myself to sleep as people do in books. But there was Victor to consider and moreover I dreaded his being ashamed of me.

First things first. Suitcases. Wherever they are they must be covered in dust by now. Where's that cloth?

At last the furtive scratch at the door that I was keyed up for. By the time he reached the kitchen I had poured his drink.

His face was set hard, then he half smiled. 'Thanks. Cheers.'

We stood awkwardly on opposite sides of the table and I thought, he's put up with enough as it is and this is the last straw. He has already decided to give me up but he doesn't know how to say it.

'Was the van right outside our gate?' I said.

'No, it never is. Next door,' he said.

'That's only half clever, isn't it?'

He flung up his shoulders and finished his drink in one mouthful and I handed him the bottle.

I wanted to put off saying it, never to have to say it in fact, but I got it out by making it sound like something else, something inconsequential. 'Your friends can give you a room, hey? Just for the meantime,' I added.

'A room? To myself? Is that your idea of a joke? Jesus, one corner of a room is wealth where they live,' and he took the bottle with him to the bedroom. When I came in he was sitting on the edge of the bed examining the ceiling. In the turned up whites of his eyes you could see the impatience and bitterness.

'What a damned nuisance those cops are, we'll have to give

up this house now,' I said.

'Do you think I don't know that?' he said irritably.

'I didn't mean to – '

'There are certain times when I actually know what has to be done, believe it or not. And without troubling you too much I might even be able to do it.'

I fiddled about in a drawer, a blur of shirts. Somehow a pullover had strayed into the wrong drawer. What does one do, leave it there?

The balls of his fingers barely touched the back of my neck. 'Sorry, hey.'

'The bastards,' I said.

'Hey,' he whistled, 'no crying. They'll come back for more if they know they can make you cry.'

I held on to him and then it passed.

'Did they give you a rough time?' he said.

'I was worried that there was no van outside, that's all.'

'I would've smelt them a mile off. You know that smell?'

I laughed into his shoulder. 'I'm beginning to.'

Then I brought down his case from the roof of the wardrobe. 'We're well ahead of them, even now,' I said. 'Talk about confusion in the ranks. They aren't even sure who they're looking for. Is it Simon Dube, the myth who insists on remaining a myth, or is it a Davis Cup star with the trickiest drop shot since Hoad? Or can it be a whole nest of incendiaries who meet here to make bombs out of caustic soda and pen nibs?'

While Victor got his things together I made coffee and corned beef sandwiches and opened our last bottle of sparkling wine. I had a brainwave and searched the cupboards and found an inch of Van der Hum in a bottle left by our landlord that was patterned, now, with delicate cobwebs. I carried everything in on two trays, it looked quite festive. The bedspread became our picnic rug.

While we ate and drank and made jokes I'm sure separate trains of thought divided us. 'Bugger it, our luck can't be that bad,' I said at one stage and ran outside to the garage to check the petrol gauge.

'It's all right, it's nearly half full,' I said when I came back into the room and Victor said, 'That bloody stupid best friend of mine, Theo, he's a fool. Shouting his mouth off to the wrong sort of people.'

'Theo?'

'He doesn't mean any harm. He gets some sort of kick out of it. Doesn't help us though.'

'When did you hear this?'

'I didn't. No one says anything directly. But there's a feeling. It wasn't there before. The supervisor knows something's going on. I can tell from the way he looks at me.'

Nothing but upsets these days. Damn Theo. 'Maybe you're imagining things,' I said.

Victor was ready hours before it was time to go. We had decided to wait till we could merge ourselves in the early morning traffic from the townships. Meanwhile we finished the wine and the liqueur but neither of us was hungry. We went outside at four o'clock and I expected to see a grainy patch in the sky where the dawn would break through but everything was pitch black still. The icy air cut across our hot faces and I thought, only a month till midsummer's day, this isn't funny. I said to Victor, 'This lousy country. Even the climate's going to pot.'

He dumped his case on the back seat. 'It'll be a hundred in the shade in a day or two, it's always like that. Nothing lasts here.'

We smiled at each other and another kind of chill streaked right through me. Nothing lasts.

'Leave the gate open, what the hell,' I said.

All around us the suburbs slept. We saw no one until a nightwatchman padded into the light at the gateway of a big Moorish house and, as my eye caught him, he yawned and pummelled his crotch. Black balls – and, how inappropriate, I blushed in the darkness at the image this conjured up.

'Do you think you should get down on the floor?' I asked.

'I refuse.'

'Good for you.'

We drove through the centre of the city in which scruffy neon lights turned the streets into a deserted fairground. On the slimy south side of the city signs of life appeared, only the signs might just as well have been those of death. Mineworkers strolled listlessly in file towards a shaft. No one seemed to be leading them there but they carried on just the same. Putting your head in the sand was nothing compared to one's daily habit of keeping it well down under the bedclothes till the sun was up.

I said to Victor, 'Are you a dawn person or a sunset person? You can't be both.'

'I'll settle for the noonday sun.'

'Any place in particular?'

'Naturally. A beach in Beira, Mozambique.'

'It was damn nice there, wasn't it.'

The road went straight ahead to the townships. The city had had no option but to build a fine paved road, monumental, otherwise the workers would never have got to their jobs on time and what would have happened to the city in that case? A grimy light shifted now behind the sky and the buses were on their way, lumbering towards us, then at the last minute pulling over, one after the other. Faces at the windows, but not really faces. Miles of smudges with hats on. Parallel to the road but out of sight behind mine dumps trains rocked along in the same direction. Dingy though the world looked in the early morning, it was good to be in the swim of things again after the long night.

'You'll be all right, hey? What happens if they can't take you in?'

'They'll fit me in, you don't know them.'

'If you've left anything behind, I'll send it down to the studio. Have you got your razor?'

'Everything's in there somewhere.'

'I'll phone you at three. Will you be in by three?'

'Should be. You can always leave a message.'

'I'll find somewhere else for us to live, I'll start today. Just for a month or so. Dick should have good news for us any day now. They'll never find us. We're much too clever for them, what do you say? They're probably in Tzaneen by now, looking under every stone for Simon Dube.'

'What about the lease? The agent won't be too pleased.'

'We can't please everyone.'

'The next gate,' Victor said.

I swung off the road into stones and dust and milk cartons. Figures marched through the archway as if in battle formation. A light still glowed in the control office and the army passed it and reached the bus stop and another army came up behind them.

If your face were black you could hide yourself in that army and never be found out.

In my mind's eye the archway turned itself into a tunnel. A place where he could crawl but not I. They let them have the ugly places, the splendid places are kept for us. He is admitted to our place when it suits us.

It sunk in all at once. I would sleep alone tonight. For, say, ninety-five per cent of my life I had slept alone. The last five per cent, however, invalidated the rest. Frequently in the middle of the night I would put out a finger to inspect the rather elusive texture of his skin. I might fold my hand over his cock, limp, now, but not flabby. Flabbiness comes to men's cocks in about their fifties, doesn't it? Tonight I would no doubt mourn for his cock. You can't even hold rights over a person's cock these days.

'How far to your friends' house?' I said.

'Not to worry. I'll get there.'

Victor's face rested in the window and I remembered Beira when I was drunk and sleepy and his face withdrew from the window and he walked back across the square to listen to the rest of what dreary old Henry O'Connell had to say.

'Keep your eye on the road. You'll be with the traffic on the way back,' he said.

Are you or are you not coming down for Christmas? my mother asked. Yes I am, I told you, I said. What a dreadful line, can't you speak up? she said. Yes of course I'm coming, I said. Marvellous, she said, that makes eighteen and so now I know where I am, I'll definitely have to get some more wine glasses. Eigh*teen*? I said. Well, the aunts for a start, she said. And the Fortescues and the Parkers had friends out from England. Now you aren't going to change your mind at the last minute? she said.

The deep mists in those hills where she lived brought out a fungus on the trees and beneath them ferns billowed in the moist light. Water slid over rocks all day long, you could see the moss growing under your eyes. Far back in the shade the blurred humps of colour turned out to be our azaleas. For the first time in months I ached all over to be there again. I couldn't explain it, yet the need persisted. Parents are incomprehensible as they grow older. Quite arbitrarily they decide what it is they want – they turn to their children again. Their children go to them. But no sooner is this accomplished than they hint that their children are doing them a favour by falling in with their wishes. I kept on wondering why parents couldn't conceive of their children burning with desire to be with them again, even though this might be only a passing phase brought on by circumstances which make parents the only people who will do.

Christmas is a Tuesday this year so they'll probably let us off at midday Monday, I said. Oh do insist, my mother said. There'll be nothing much going on in the office anyway, I said.

Don't break your neck, but do you think you could be here in time for midnight Mass? she said. We could all go together. She had promised her hydrangeas for the altar, she said.

Afterwards I spoke to Dick's secretary on the office line.

Any news from London office? I asked. About the scholarship, I had to remind her.

Yes, she'd seen a telex. But to be quite honest she couldn't recall what they'd said. The boss hadn't passed it back for filing yet.

Oh it wasn't urgent, I said, I'd phone again next week.

Bye now, she said, and I began to worry about the weeks passing and nothing happening.

At one o'clock sharp I went up to the corner to get the first edition of the newspapers. It was streaming with rain. I ran back to the office through the rain and shut my door and spread the newspapers on my desk and traced through the smalls columns with a ballpoint pen to make little crosses here and there. The districts I selected were the ramshackle ones on the downtown edge. Three or four houses sounded just right and I telephoned the agents and made appointments for after five.

I drove round in the rain and chose a house. From the kitchen door you could see the stained glass windows behind the high altar of the Catholic cathedral which looked like a wedding cake giving way at the seams in the rain. The rain sloshed down into the backyard and the rims of puddles tipped and flowed together and deepened between the two tin fences. There was no sign of a gutter in which to drain away. At my shoulder the agent coughed. He pointed out that the kitchen had recently been repainted. But the yard makes the place. I couldn't tell him this. As long as those high tin fences stood up to the rain our cave was intact, so who cared that the single coat of gloss on the kitchen walls was fresh or otherwise?

Bit of paint here, bit of plaster there, well, he said, it's a proposition.

I wasn't buying the house, I made it clear to him.

An odour of damp sand hung over the neighbourhood. The backs of so many little cringing houses and, on the ridge above us, the slender columns of apartment blocks like the outline of a faraway city in the rain.

To impress on the agent that my head wasn't quite in the clouds, I inspected once more two tiny dark bedrooms, a dark living room and a slit of a bathroom in which a gas cylinder must once have exploded. The roof didn't leak and the rent was low and no one I knew lived for miles around. Between the front door and the fence there was just enough space for two sodden dahlias.

Occupation on the first of the month, we agreed.

What with having to pay a month's rent in advance I couldn't scrape up more than half a month's rent as a sort of recompense, or conscience money, for moving out of the other house without proper notice. I spoke to Victor on the telephone but he wouldn't see me and I did not press him. His voice gave nothing away, I had only my own fears to guide me. He's had time now to weigh it all up and it isn't worth it any more, it's as simple as that. I told myself this as his voice on the radio in the empty house induced a hard-on and a sore heart simultaneously.

I ate eggs and lived out of suitcases, having packed my things the day he left as evidence that I was staying on in the house not because of choice but by necessity. I hated the house. Without looking to left or right I moved between kitchen, bathroom and bedroom. I drank too much and had frightening dreams. I could not piece the dreams together in the morning.

I kept away from everyone, I wanted to live from day to day without being put off my stroke. Frankie and Geoff left messages, which I stored in various drawers. I did not trust myself to stand out against other people's affection and advice.

Soon voices could be heard bellowing with relief, yes, there's no doubt about it now, the drought's broken. And so the maize crop was saved, next year's citrus exports might well set a new record, the stock market had no excuse for not roaring ahead again.

Rain rustled on the roof all night long. Fallen jacaranda flowers massed into pulp in the path and my drain was blocked. Weeds sprouted on the tennis court and I felt ashamed of my lethargy, but not seriously enough to want to do anything about it.

I was living in the house behind the cathedral. Victor knew this but would not come to the house. Move in over the weekend, I told him, but he said no, thanks all the same, and I left it at that.

Then he telephoned me from a call box and said he would be at Siegfried's that day. I did not know what to expect. I started a press release on coal output, then put it aside and went to Siegfried's.

Victor looked up when I walked in but he did not come across to me. He was at a table with Hazel and Theo and two or three others whose faces I recalled from the show but their names were lost. Siegfried's smile blazed slightly off centre as usual and he slung an arm round my shoulder and steered me too expansively to a corner table.

'Reserved for Mr V Butele and A N Other. Now we know it's none other than *the* Mr A N Other.'

'Who else did you think it might be?'

'Me? I never ask questions, especially to myself.'

'No wonder you've got such a good business here.'

He propped a foot on the crossbar of my chair and grinned into my face. You should wear an eyepatch, it would complete the picture, I thought. I think he knew I distrusted him, but this did not touch him either way.

'Long time no see.'

'Been away.'

'Business or pleasure?'

'I thought you said you never ask questions.'

His laughter went on and on. 'I forget the answers anyway,' he said.

Then two men came clinking through the seashell curtain,

one of them white, and he breathed in my ear, 'From *The Times* of London. They said for me to expect him. They all come here.'

I lit a cigarette. I couldn't understand why I was being made to sit there by myself.

Hazel said, 'Hi stranger,' and dropped down opposite me.

She wore a shiny white raincoat and her eyes were strangely lit.

'So the tour's over. You must miss the show,' I said.

They might go on to London, she said. And if London, why not New York? They were waiting to hear from either one of two managements.

Cape Town went wild over them, the tour ended there. 'I met a friend of yours,' she said. 'He sings leads with that opera group. What a voice.'

'So they say.'

'He said to give his regards. He forgot your name. But he said I'd recognise you. Give my regards to the handsomest boy in town.'

'That was last year.'

'You mean you're not in the running any more?'

I smiled across at her, her earnest tone bewildered me.

'Don't talk about running,' I said.

Hazel placed her curiously stumpy hands palms down on the table. 'For a long time what I been wanting to tell you is this. You must let go of Victor. But I'm saying it too late now and I don't know what to say that's best for him.'

Why did she talk about being too late? I asked her.

'He has lost his job,' she said.

'They gave him the sack?'

She shook her shoulders impatiently. 'He resigned. But it's the same thing in the end. He couldn't go on working there with all that gossip. Like being on top of a time bomb day in and day out.' Hazel lifted her eyes and I watched them coldly looking me over. 'He gave up his job on account of you,' she said.

Bit by bit I saw the shape of things, and I said, 'You hate me, you really do.'

She grabbed a cigarette from my pack and swiftly lit it. 'No, I haven't got it in me to hate like that.'

'But you disapprove and you have your reasons. The main reason, and I suppose it's the only one that counts really, is that I'm white. And this means I think I can have whatever I want and generally mess around and then get away free when the time comes.'

'I told you, I don't hate like that. But maybe there's some truth in what you say. Seems to me you have everything on your side and he has stood by you and lost out. No person likes to see waste. Waste is for the birds, I'm telling you.'

'What does he want to do now?' I said after a while.

Hazel let the smoke drift in front of her face. She laughed softly. 'You and he are the ones who must work it out, hey!'

'Everything I've done – ' I started.

'Go on,' said Hazel.

'I don't have to defend myself to you,' I said, knowing this to be childish, but not minding once I'd said it. It shifted some of the fog in my own head, for one thing. Maybe sincerity in love wasn't enough after all. One must cut oneself out of the action from time to time and study it from a distance, coolly and cleverly. I had not done this, it had never occurred to me to do so.

Hazel picked at her scarf, which she then folded inside the V of her raincoat again. 'One thing to be said for you. You don't beat a drum for us blacks so as to make yourself feel better inside. You aren't a fake liberal, I'll say that for you.'

'Maybe I should be, then there wouldn't be such a mess. But it doesn't seem to take me that way. It's just that there's only one person I want to be with all the time.'

When she had gone back to her table I thought possibly this was how he intended to leave things meanwhile and that it was time I went and he could get in touch with me when he was ready. From his point of view, his being ready must coincide, of course, with my having shed some of my heat, preferably all of it. Then he wouldn't object in the least to our starting up again on some other axis, a passionless one. Just buddies, okay?

He fell into the chair next to me. He hadn't shaved that day and his face looked shabby. Those wretched instincts of mine that behave like tentacles reared up again without a second's pause.

'We better order. The service here's gone to hell,' he said.

I tried to conceal the concern I felt and I must have succeeded because his smile did not die away. He was pleased to see me, he said. 'Do you have to be back at two sharp?' he said.

'They should manage to hold out till two-thirty,' I said.

'Working hard?'

'Half-half.'

He suggested the chops because they wouldn't take long. Siegfried bounced up, then away again fortunately. Between his jittery arms I caught sight of Theo across the room and we waved but that was all for the moment.

'Been looking after yourself?' Victor said.

'That's easy,' I said. Except that I couldn't sleep, I said. 'I've got these sensational pills. They're purple and pink. More purple than pink really. You can get through exactly two pages of any book – doesn't matter which author – and then they hit you over the head, clonk. Only trouble is in the morning you need a crane to get you out of bed again.'

'You must give them up,' he said.

He asked me about the move. He headed me off when I tried to slip in a question about how it was in the township with his friends.

The new house was one size up from a doll's house, you couldn't swing a cat in it, I told him.

But since when did we treat our pets like that anyway? he said.

It struck me all over again that he was the most interesting man I had ever known and that a certain vision he possessed made so much of what he said worth remembering.

When we had finished our chops we drank spineless instant coffee but it was like champagne to me because Victor had just said he would meet me after work.

'Where're your things?' I said.

He pointed towards the kitchen.

'Unless they've put them in the goddam stew by now,' he said.

The tiredness and despair lived in the marrow of his bones and he could no longer disguise this.

Soon afterwards there was a cloudburst and then the sky cleared, as so often happened in Johannesburg on those summer afternoons. The sun licked up the dark puddles streaky with oil and people streamed out of the city towards the suburbs. I found Victor behind the curtain at Siegfried's. He had been drinking with Siegfried during the afternoon. He did this both to forget and to unwind himself.

Inside the front door of our house he let his suitcase fall and pulled me against him without saying a word. 'The world is a fine place,' he said later on. 'If only we didn't have to live in it.' Then he said, 'I missed you, I bet I missed you more than you missed me.'

I purposely did not speak because hot on the last syllable of the first word would have followed the howls of a mindless crybaby and it was enough for the moment to let our bodies carry the message. We held on to each other beneath a very depressing light fitting of orange plastic and I knew that for Victor, from now on, making love would correspond with oblivion and that this was all he required of it.

The house delighted him, in particular the walls of the house that surrounded us, shutting out everything else. Privacy was a privilege that bowled him over, like some fresh experience. Merely by swinging his eyes over the house he converted it into a palace.

'You're a clever kid. No more compliments. What do we do next?'

I said, 'The front bedroom's one square foot bigger but from this one you can lie in bed and keep an eye on the cathedral.'

Victor put his clothes away, it was all done in a few minutes.

I switched on the gas stove, breathing in that first rather intoxicating whiff, then lit it. Victor stood beside me, I could hardly believe it.

'It's too hot for steak. How about ham and tongue and salads and I'll make that dressing?' I said.

He agreed, and I turned off the gas and then we strolled through the low dark stuffy rooms again. We settled down near the front door to catch the breeze. The door was half ajar so we were hidden from the street and we kept the lights off.

'Welcome to the district.'

We raised our glasses and Victor's smile showed for an instant in the darkness. 'Brandy's good for the constitution, I'm not kidding.'

Outside in the street children screamed racing to and fro. Immigration from southern Europe was gathering pace again and this was a district which they could afford and where they felt at home, a long way from open spaces. After twenty years they would have moved either to one of the prim new suburbs or back to Cyprus, depending on why they had come to Africa in the first place.

When the silence between us had gone on for a long time, I said, 'We've had our first caller. She's half Afrikaans, half Greek and married to a Neapolitan house painter. She came in yesterday to ask if her husband could repaint the roof. Seems like he's gone to seed in the tropics and it's over to her to pull in the contracts. She wants to get on in the world. She despises her neighbour's language. Man, it's bad for the children. You know how kids like short words. The Portuguese are the worst of the lot. She says the fruit shop at the corner is the local whorehouse. The Portuguese men leave their wives behind in

Oporto, so they keep black whores behind the lettuces. Mister, she said, people just don't know what goes on around here and those police know less. Her name is Alma.'

The rotted dahlia smell leaked through the doorway and I glanced out at the street lights and the torn pavements. Children still floated up and down under the lights but they were quieter now.

The air was close and I put on shorts and mixed the salad dressing in the kitchen. Victor followed me around, then he perched on the table next to the coffee cup without a handle that I was using instead of a bowl. The skin of his face was like old leaves. An iron tonic (but there's a special name for it) will fix that in no time and I'll have good news for you one of these days, I was thinking.

With an abruptness he could never master he grabbed my hand, knocking the spoon aside. His eyes stared down as he ground my knuckles one against the other. I held his hand and said, as though we had only recently met and everything had to be explained from the beginning, 'Ag, don't worry, you mustn't worry. Nothing that happens can change what I feel.'

'Yes, I know that now and it bothers me,' he said.

Dick did not tell me face to face. His secretary's voice came through on the office line, then I heard him saying, 'Disappointing news, I'm afraid.'

'That's one way of starting a conversation,' I said, and I tried to laugh.

'London dug up some interesting stuff on broadcasting, but a mezzo is the lucky girl this year. The committee has just come in with its decision,' he said.

'Oh,' I said. I went on, 'Don't you think the Organisation's big enough and rich enough to afford *two* scholarships a year?'

'Funny you should say that. I'd decided to recommend it myself.'

'Marvellous,' I said, or some such sound.

'Of course it takes a bit of time. Board approval, that sort of thing. But they'll agree in the end, have no fear.'

I said, 'I've just seen the first proofs of the annual report. The Organisation made a profit of twenty-seven million rands last year.'

Just the faintest suggestion of a critical laugh. 'Now now, Ray, keep your hair on. You're one of us after all, aren't you?'

'Sorry. But your tests are a bit tough sometimes,' I said, intending that this should go deep with him.

'I see no reason why Victor shouldn't get it next year. Will you remember this?'

'If I don't, perhaps nobody will.'

He let this pass, and his reasons for doing so were his own, and he said, 'This mezzo is evidently something quite special. She's been in the queue for a couple of years.'

'She deserves it then.'

'And when are we seeing you again? I'll get Margaret to give you a ring. You fix a date with Victor. We'll all drink a toast to next year.'

'Yes,' I said.

'Margaret feels you've been neglecting her lately,' he said.

'Been a bit tied up.'

'You know how Margaret exaggerates,' he said.

4

Rain fell at night and then the sun rose in a cloudless sky, it was wonderful to see. I slid out of bed, Victor did not stir. I looked out the window at the rinsed blue sky. I opened the kitchen door waiting for the kettle to boil. The sun reached the cathedral windows and I thought how lovely they must look inside with the sun sailing through them. I had never been into the cathedral, I had no urge to do so. I sat on the sink and drank coffee slowly and let any number of pleasant thoughts take over. They had come and gone before I could pin them down.

Victor was so sound asleep I went to shave before making fresh coffee for him. I had not broken the news yet about the scholarship.

I'll tell him when I take in his coffee. I started soaping my chin.

No I won't, I'll tell him tonight over drinks.

A week had passed since Dick had told me the mezzo was the winner.

Maybe she'll turn it down, or get polio.

A curl of shaving cream crept up my nose. I bit back the sneeze.

I don't think Dick tried hard enough. Why didn't he? Or am I being unfair?

I had no talent in those days for acknowledging disappointment in my friends.

Definitely tonight. Over drinks. When we're halfway through our third. Quite casually. And we need never refer to it again.

On the way to work I would be calling in at the AA to get a road map. Was it the anticipation of having the map in my hands that made me feel so happy?

I put on my almost black grey suit, which was my favourite. I took in Victor's coffee. He opened his eyes and sat up. He said, 'Dressed already?'

'What do you mean, already?'

He looked glumly at me. 'I'll work again one day and we'll be rich like before, you watch.'

'Don't let's start on that again. Drink your coffee,' I said.

'How's life?' he said.

'It's the most fantastic day,' I said.

'Thanks.' He took his cup but waited for the coffee to cool. He slept naked in the summer, his body showed up at its startling best among white sheets and pillows.

'What do your cards say for you today?' he said.

'Background story on zinc. Imagine it.'

I went back to the kitchen to check on our brandy. Victor needed it, though we never spoke about this. As long as it was there, he could get through the day. This would all change once we had left Africa, I told myself.

'Here,' I said, 'vitamin Q.' I gave him a pear and a knife and sat on the bed. He put the pear and knife aside for the time being. He drew me down and I lay next to him in my suit and black shoes. We were quite still for several minutes. I could not recall our having been like this before, not at eight o'clock in the morning with me all dressed up.

Down at the corner the bus grunted as it took off again. I stood up most unwillingly and crossed to the door, making a bit of play of dragging my feet along the floorboards. Victor smiled quite cheerfully from the bed but, as far as I remember, he did not have anything more to say.

'See you,' I said, 'at 5.18.'

I left the house. I walked faster than usual towards the park in an attempt to shake off the queer feeling that had come over me as if from nowhere. He's depressed because he's out of a job and time drags and this morning you've caught it from him, that's all it amounts to.

Our district of moth-eaten houses dropped away at the end of the block. In the park the standard roses were trimmed and petted to look like beauties of long ago with pouting bosoms that sloped down to tiny ankles. Behind the blunt privet hedge I heard children already screaming their heads off on the trampoline.

I hurried through the light and shade under the oak trees and then the city began. I loved walking to work, it brought Johannesburg within a different dimension, rather a foreign one.

I came out of the AA with the map, of Swaziland and its frontier with the Transvaal, caught into a roll by a rubber band. As I was not a member I had not had to sign for it but had paid for it, like you would with a cash sale in a shop, anonymously.

The morning grew even more beautiful as the sun brightened, making cool black shadows on the sides of buildings. After twenty-five minutes I reached the office. The custom in our department was to shout hello as you passed each doorway. I did this, then closed my door and phoned Len Silver in order to ask him to meet me either today or tomorrow, as soon as he could. He would put me right on the best route into Swaziland, away from the border posts. He wasn't in yet. I left my number.

The background to zinc mining was so dull it calmed me down. While I was hanging out the open window for a second or two I looked down and there was Dick passing by the fountain in a brown suit. Perhaps it was my yellow hair that caught his eye and made him glance up. He waved rather sedately and I waved back before he went on his way.

At last the morning was over. A group of us rode up in the lift to the canteen. A few months before the country had changed from pounds, shillings and pence to the decimal system and the personnel department had issued new ten cent lunch tickets. One of our group pulled an old one shilling ticket from his hip pocket, he wondered whether he would be allowed to use it. Someone with playful eyes said, 'Not to worry, they've kept back some of the old meals.' People in the lift thought I'd had a fit as I dropped to my knees and came up with tears of laughter turning all the faces around me into fishes swaying to and fro behind glass. The man who had spoken made me sit with him at lunch. He wanted someone to know that his ambition in life was to live on top of a hill in San Francisco looking down day and night on the bridges and the bay.

The afternoon passed so slowly you could hear time sliding by. I tried again to get hold of Len Silver. Yes, he was in for a bit, but he's out again. I told the girl we closed at five and it was urgent. Give me your home number, she rapped out. Then she said it wasn't her fault if I had no phone in the house. I saw a bad omen in everything now. Forget it, I'll use the call box at the corner, I told her. Maybe you'll catch him, she said, maybe not.

I walked home with the evening sun behind me heating my neck. People spun this way and that in the crowded shadowy streets and I played a game with myself, and with them, by pretending to hold on to the Swaziland map inattentively, as though it meant nothing more to me than the evening paper. Is there anyone else walking home with a map in his hand? A strip map to Cape Town perhaps. Which way shall we go this year? Via Bloemfontein or Kimberley? Same mileage more or less. Let's give the kids their first sight of the Big Hole at Kimberley. First night's stop at Beaufort West. The motel where there's a dormitory for the servants. The next afternoon the sea again. My God how I need this holiday.

I came back to earth, my hands shivering. But – don't be a cunt. Lots of time for holidays later on. You've made your decision. Don't go back on your decision. Once made, you must stick to it.

I passed through the park and ran into the house where Victor was standing aimlessly between two doors.

'How's Frank?' he said.

'No idea.'

'Born liar. You had lunch with him.'

'No,' I said, 'I didn't.'

'You've been looking forward to having lunch with him all week, I could tell.'

I pitched my jacket into a chair. I thought I saw dust rising out of the chair.

'How's Geoff?'

'Must be all right. If he wasn't we'd have heard presumably.'

'You're sure you haven't seen him?'

'No. I mean yes. I haven't seen him.'

'One doesn't know whether to believe you or not.'

I looked into his eyes feeling useless and sad and hoping I would find Len Silver tonight.

He said, 'You're still smoking too much.'

I went into our bedroom, glad to be away from his eyes for a minute or two. The sunset light on the ice cream cathedral waved madly up and down our bed. I pushed away my shoes and socks and put on jeans.

'Sundowners,' I called, making for the kitchen.

He was a tidy drinker, even at this stage. His glass, rinsed and dried, was back in the cupboard. There was still enough brandy left for tonight.

In France we'll live on Courvoisier. After Malaga we will go to France to settle down.

The back of the dahlia's head was drying out and I caught the papery odour as we quickly drank brandy on kitchen chairs inside the front door. To Malaga via Swaziland. From Johannesburg to Swaziland to Lourenço Marques to Luanda to Lisbon to Malaga. But first I must speak to Len Silver. I must get it all straight in my own mind. Then money. A loan from Geoff. One-way tickets. Half the price of a return ticket plus ten per cent. Or is it twelve and a half? When everything is fixed I'll sweep Victor off his feet.

He said, 'What is your feeling for me based on?'

'Listen here,' I said. 'Let's have one night without a fight.'

'Could it be kindness of heart? Or softening of the arteries? Or self-conceit or lack of willpower?'

'You're a bore. You weren't always a bore.'

'There's so much about you I can't work out. I can't stand what I can't work out. I can't stand your outbursts of sincerity. Your innocence and enthusiasm, I can't stand all the rubbish in your character.'

'I'm just one of those dull characters who has a job.'

'Shit pun,' he said.

He said, 'Don't think I'm trying to make you out as an enigma or anything. You're not complex. You're just good at acting a part for a certain time.'

There was something cheering about his point of view. It told me he wasn't nearly finished, there was lots of fight left in him. The last man in the world to be beaten into mush would be Victor Butele. I was happy now to know I was no longer afraid of him. The time had not quite arrived, however, when he could be told this.

I said, 'How hungry are you?'

'The usual.'

'That all?'

But his thoughts were elsewhere already, so I went away through the darkening house into the kitchen. Far away thunder barked in the sky above some distant town. I stuck cloves into pork chops.

After we had eaten in silence I told him I was going out.

'Aren't you lucky.'

'Is that really your opinion?'

'You never pay attention to my opinion anyway.'

'I'm going to the call box,' I said.

He studied me above his clenched knuckles. 'Okay, I believe you.'

The left-over stink of cigarette smoke in call boxes has a high heady quality. I shoved my foot in the door to let in air while I dialled Len Silver's number. As soon as I heard his voice I took my foot away and curled my hand round the mouthpiece.

He couldn't come tonight, he said.

'Just half an hour. Ten minutes. Come as late as you like.'

Out of the question. He seemed to have doubts about my phoning him at all.

'Tomorrow night? How about lunch tomorrow?'

He seemed to be weighing it all up.

He wants to make sure I realise that, against all the rules, I've butted in.

'Please. There isn't anyone else I can talk to.'

He got it out with an impassive grunt. Tomorrow night at nine. Where? he said.

'In Doornfontein. It's easy to find. Come down Harrow Road to Saratoga.'

He listened, then asked what I was doing living in that area. He did not associate me with the area, he said.

'Rents are low,' I said.

He knew that, he said. But ...

'You'll see why tomorrow,' I said.

Trouble? he asked.

'Yes, I suppose so.'

But I had good connections. Why turn to him? he laughed harshly.

His laugh made me feel more isolated than ever. I must not let him get a rise out of me though, I must let him say whatever he feels is right. 'What do you drink?' I said.

With an utterly different laugh this time: 'Beer and dog biscuits.'

Get a good night's sleep, he said unexpectedly.

The shredded pavements tickled my bare feet under the sooty little oak trees. Something in a grey robe smelling of wine passed quite close to me and at the same moment an uproar started in the house with tin walls at the top of the street. In a few seconds it was all over. I stood inside our front door scraping the sweat off my face.

'Hey, Victor.'

I found him in bed in the dark and he held me by the upper arm and then traced a line from my shoulder to my wrist again and again. He laughed whenever he came to the horny cap of skin on my elbow. No matter the weather, damp or dry, I could not get rid of it.

'How often must I tell you? Vaseline and candle wax. An old nigger recipe,' he said.

'Tomorrow,' I said.

I wanted us to make love, so that we would both sleep. The nagging fear, however, was that his body might be bored to death with mine. I lowered a hand until his balls filled it. The greatest crap in the world is that a ball is a ball is a ball. If a pair of balls is the wrong weight, shape, balance, you do not seek them out a second time. Victor's were fine, for me anyhow. And the language was not worn out after all. I knew that sigh well. It set me off, as it had always done. The warmth of his balls in my hand stayed on after he had moved above me.

I woke later on and shifted over to my own pillow and occasionally noted contrasting layers of darkness on the ceiling through half-closed eyes. I could hear nothing but Victor's gloomy cough close beside me. I touched the side of his hip as my thoughts turned towards rivers slipping out of mountains and I dreamed of rivers flushing through glassy valleys to the sea and I fell asleep again.

At first it was like having a third person in the room with us. I did not have to open my eyes to know that this person was already there. The person took the form of a smudge of light that hopped and skipped behind my eyelids. I opened my eyes at the moment that the light swerved abruptly on to the sheet. So it wasn't a light disguising itself as a smudge in a dream after all. The presence changed shape as the white sheet blazed where my feet stuck up under it. I think I knew then that the dream had passed. All the same I did not move. I simply lay there waiting. A second later the torchlight blinded me.

When it lost its bite it was only because it had swept aside to bear down on Victor. I rubbed the lilac and silver and black spangles out of my eyes. Their delicate but dulled rims remained inside my lids, they even hurt a little. I sat up.

In the shot of light Victor shielded his eyes and glanced sideways at me through his fingers from the pillow. His reaction was still paced by whatever dream he had come out of. Alternatively he was wide awake and determined to keep up some form of dignity.

At last a voice, even though the most horrid one in our experience.

'Maak oop.'

'What's the bet they aren't going to switch off their torch,' I said.

Time went by. We stayed where we were, caught by the light on us.

Without warning Victor ripped off the sheet. We both stared straight ahead into the funnel of light from the window. An extraordinary silence built up on the other side of the window.

Perhaps they've melted away in embarrassment. Or has none of this really happened yet? That light is nothing but an hallucination affecting both of us simultaneously.

'Maak oop.'

And so I got out of bed and looked around for something to put on. Until I left home I always had dressing gowns, silk for summer, wool for winter. I came from a world in which the whole household had beautiful dressing gowns. Somehow dressing gowns had vanished from my life. I found my jeans after a while.

'Yes?'

I stood in the kitchen doorway so that none of them could pass me without pushing me aside.

'Afrikaans of Engels?' Someone was asking the usual first question.

I recognised the greenish face of the detective in the crowd.

'As I said last time, dit maak nie saak nie.'

The prologue is always the same: one's answers aren't listened to.

'Now we will enter,' the detective said.

I stuck out my hand, palm upwards, waiting.

He jerked his head towards the man next to him. 'No warrant is required,' he said.

There were five of them. The detective and the one from security police wore soup-coloured sports jackets that rode above their arses. Two of the uniformed policemen were white, the other black. The black one looked neither aggressive nor menacing. He had simply lost touch, for the moment, with the role he was expected to play. Verdigris still flourished on the detective's jawbone.

One minute the kitchen was crammed with motionless staring figures, the next minute I was left there alone. I tried to settle on a decisive course of action, but nothing came of it. I followed the police force into the bedroom.

Victor, with a towel round him, stood dead-centre of the room surrounded by the force. In the old days at the flat I had picked up some candy-pink towels on a sale. A braid of darker pink rosebuds bordered each towel. Victor's skin gave one of these towels a distinction I had never noticed in it before.

'We will see your pass,' the detective said.

When Victor bent over a drawer the notches of his spine made a charming pattern of texture and light. I could not take my eyes off that mysterious area at the base of his spine. All of a sudden it was no longer undefined, I recognised in it his vulnerability.

The detective glanced down at Victor's pass. 'As I thought.' He handed it scornfully to one of the others. 'What did I tell you?' the security policeman dropped the pass into a briefcase.

I found a shirt hanging on the doorknob and I put it on while they all watched me. My fingers wobbled with the buttons so, rather than make an issue out of it, I shoved the shirt tail into the top of my jeans and let my eyes rise casually towards the first face within reach. The security policeman and I examined one another. One of those plump beige faces with a foxiness at its centre. The fat falls away the longer you study it.

The detective said to Victor, 'The time is 3.50 am. What are you doing in this house?'

I spoke from the doorway. 'He lives here.'

'I question the Bantu,' the detective said.

At last my mind cleared. A choice of action became easier. I am in shit street. Nevertheless I am white. I will use that privilege to protect him. You there. Listen. As long as he and I are in the same room you watch your step.

'He shares this house with me.'

'It is to the Bantu I – '

'He lives here.'

They were all facing me, now, and this gave me confidence in myself. The men in sports jackets no longer hid their loathing. As for the others, they merely followed suit in a mindless way. And so, it occurred to me, the fight as we have known it up till now is over. Then it is true what people say. One does feel a sense of relief. It's like a fresh start. Action now turns on a brand new axis.

The detective said, 'You and the Bantu will come along.'

'First I must brush my teeth.'

None of them followed me. I had the bathroom to myself. I made the most of it. I flung cold water over my face and let it evaporate on my skin to cool me down. I combed my hair and took three aspirins and crammed my eyes with Eye-gene so they would look shiny and alert and would disconcert whoever was selected to question me.

'It's all yours,' I called to Victor as I came out of the bathroom humming a tune.

All five of them still barricaded him in the bedroom. Our bed had been stripped meanwhile. Our sheets made a limp greyish pile on a chair at the door. One constable appeared to have been ordered to stand guard over the sheets. Exhibit 'A'.

The room was beginning to smell of bodies inside uniforms. They let Victor through and I smiled at the sour expressions on their faces as they heard him close the bathroom door. But surely you understand. We *live* here. Words in themselves are not quite enough though. It is only when they are fleshed out with the facts of living that the message storms through.

In the silence they heard the lavatory flush. Yes, I'm afraid we crap in the same bowl.

'Kom.'

The security man and the detective wheeled angrily into the passage. They tramped through to the sitting room and began switching on lights. It sounded as though they were hacking the house to bits in their search. Hadn't they found enough for one night? Lunn's *Revolutionary Socialism*, for example, would surely be thin meat after the catch in the bedroom. Something uncertain about their attitude puzzled me and this gave me heart, though I couldn't quite explain why it should.

The black constable vanished but the two white ones lolled in the doorway while I dressed. They moved fractionally aside to let Victor back into the room and we both put on office suits and white shirts and black shoes. I tried to catch his eye, he would not permit this. All I wanted him to know was that it had just dawned on me that, now, we would never be parted. In my crazy mind it seemed to me that the joke had ended, that reality, at last, had taken over. Oddly enough the presence of the constables was not intrusive, it was rather like having cattle peer mildly at you across a fence.

'Now we will go.'

The detective looked us up and down. I think it displeased him that we had managed to dress up while his back was turned.

'What do you keep in here?' he shouted suddenly.

He and the security policeman tore silently through the chest of drawers. I recalled specific occasions such as our visit to Victor's daughter and Margaret and Dick's party for the opera group as certain shirts and socks flipped into sight, then away, till when? My mother's reminiscences invariably turned on clothes. When the royal prince visited our town the month before my sister was born she wore fold upon fold of green sprigged chiffon and he dropped a cigarette butt right next to her at the garden party. Craven A, cork.

So, what would my parents have to say about all this?

We trooped outside. I felt a pang at leaving our rickety little house. Wiser, perhaps, for we two never to be won over by houses, carpets, dahlias in front yards. The moon slipped away behind clouds. There was rain in the air. Two vans were parked one behind the other in the street and I did not see the point of this at first. We came to a stop while the policemen whispered to one another, like the sound of snakes rustling.

'This way.'

A huge hand brushed my sleeve and I realised we were to be separated. This was the first of the really bad moments, so I made a point of smiling at Victor under the street lamp. What would they do to him on his own?

'Silly, isn't it?' I said.

He glanced across at the two vans and I noticed he was starting to smile too. A second black policeman stepped into the lamplight. We made quite a crowd in the little street. The crowd broke up into two groups. I am a member of the white group, at this and all other times. Victor is a member of the black group, of which there are subgroups, or tribes, with names like Xhosa, Zulu, Sotho (northern and southern), Tembu, Shangaan. Neither of us feels himself to be a solid proud member of his group, but this is irrelevant as matters stand.

I busied myself with this jumble of thoughts as we were led to the two vans. My father's point of view is, who pays for all this madness – we poor bloody whites, who else?

The doors of Victor's van banged shut. It drove away ahead of us. I made a note of this. I identified the devil's work in each fragment of the action. At last we followed. I think it was the detective and one of the policemen who sat on either side of me in the back of the van. I tried to plot our route, which no doubt is what most people do when riding along in one of these vans. While we were still in the house I did not feel I was a different person to the one I was yesterday. It must have been the impact of the interior of that van that marked the division. So the world is as simple as that, is it? There are the poor and the rich, the mad and the sane, those who have broken laws and those who have broken them but who have not been found out.

I was afraid but I knew I must conceal this, particularly from myself. I must not rush into any decisions yet. It seems to me all one's mistakes are made because one is afraid.

When the van stopped we got out. No one spoke, I longed for a cigarette. We were in a courtyard with high dark walls on all sides. I looked around for Victor's van and, when there was no sign of it, I was about to say something. The detective stared coldly at me though, so I turned aside. They have a master plan to break us down individually, I thought. Pretend you have no strong feelings in the matter.

'Walk here,' the detective said.

The security policeman stayed close beside me. I had no idea where we were. I hated leaving the open air and having to go inside that building. Passages with no one in them darted this way and that but eventually we reached an immense charge office brilliantly lit and full of policemen chattering away behind a counter. So it was Central Square after all. I felt quite cheered up, the ground under me seemed a little firmer. How often I had peered into this charge office from the other world of the street outside. It had a rather impromptu air about it in the daylight. At the end of the counter was a section where you could pay traffic fines. More than once I had seen people I knew bustling in with their chequebooks. The only emotion they showed was annoyance.

I slowed down, but the security policeman shook his head. Behind the counter faces looked up sideways. A weird silence took over. Four am brought in the special cases, the drunks had been rounded up hours ago. We went up through the heart of the building in a grey steel lift. I counted five floors when the lift doors shot open.

I was led into a room, not a cell. They made me hand over my watch for some reason.

'May I smoke?' I said.

'No,' said the security policeman and he took my cigarettes and lighter and he and the detective went away.

A policeman in uniform appeared instantly and sat on a chair inside the door.

'Why can't I smoke?' I said.

The policeman stared through me with muddy eyes. On the sides of his cheeks the blackheads he had once rooted out had left behind a honeycomb of tiny holes.

There were three or four office chairs and a table with a solitary ink-stain and an empty bookshelf. The police station was named after the Prime Minister though most people still called it Central Square, the name of the earlier more raffish headquarters on the same site. An airport, a four-lane highway and a dam had also been given the name of this Prime Minister.

I concentrated my thoughts on salami for a few minutes and my craving for a cigarette faded away slightly.

I was so glad to see light beginning to show in the sky. Rain drifted against the window pane and far away beyond the rain I could just make out a steely stain in the sky. What would they charge us with? I had no idea whether the Immorality Act applied to a pair of men as well as to men and women. The men and women cases always followed the same course, according to a journalist I had once known. The same as in rape cases, he told me. When the policeman is called into court he provides the climactic evidence against which there can be no argument. Ja, naturally he examined the man. He says, 'Sy privaat was nat.' Seven years for the man with the wet cock.

How we laughed – Afrikaans gave it such a buffoonish cast. Tell it in English and you wouldn't raise a smile. Too close to home perhaps? Or was it something else again – that soured defensive form of attack on which people without power invariably fall back?

I looked across at the policeman. Our eyes met, held, exchanged nothing. Where is he? was what I wanted to ask him.

Go on, tell. Let your team down.

Don't you ever let your team down?

So I turned towards the window again and the rain had stopped. The outlines of buildings, mostly tipsy, came and went as brown mist thinned, then sailed in again.

'Have you no sense?' the detective shouted at the policeman. He barged across the room to yank down the blind in front of my face.

'Take this chair,' he said to me.

I was in the middle of the room. I had felt far safer next to the window.

The security policeman wandered into the room to sit opposite me. Another one followed him, they both faced me. The detective stood against the wall, his fingers fiddling with his lips.

'What are your politics?' I was asked.

'Where is Victor Butele?' I said.

'Reply,' they said.

'I must have my lawyer here,' I said.

'A lawyer is not necessary,' they said.

'I must speak to someone,' I said.

'There is no provision for a lawyer. Answer the question. What are your politics?'

'First you must lay a charge,' I said.

'We know what we are doing. You must answer the questions. For which party did you cast a vote in the election?'

'I didn't vote,' I said.

'Why did you not vote?'

'The poll had closed.'

'Every citizen has a duty to cast a vote.'

149

'No. You have to register your name. You don't have to vote.'

'We do not believe you did not cast a vote. Which party do you belong to?'

'I don't belong to any party.'

'Why is this so?'

'Not everyone belongs to a party.'

'Are you a member of a party that is not recognised by law?'

And so on. And then they said, 'What books. What books do you choose to read?'

I said, 'You searched once before. Whatever books you saw then, those are the ones I read.'

'You do not read only those books. We have information on other books.'

'What does it matter whether I read or not?'

'We must tell you. We have information on you. Further to the books, we have information.'

'Then what about the charge? What is the charge?'

But they hurried on, prodding vaguely at me. Through it all I knew somehow that their questions were deliberately off centre, that with these questions they were filling in time. This did not mean, however, that beneath this hesitancy they were not enraged. On whose orders, I wondered, were they waiting?

Half my mind was on Victor. Was he in a chair in a room like mine? Don't be ridiculous, they'd make him stand.

'Why do you choose to work at such a place as the Langenfelder mining group?'

'They give you a good training.'

'Training? What are they training you for?'

'It's called public relations.'

'This Langenfelder. He is dubious.'

I said, 'I don't think that's the word you're looking for.'

'Stop your cheek.' The pale crusty eyes of the second security policeman flared at me through downy white lashes. He said, 'This Langenfelder of yours, he is not a patriot.'

The other one said, 'Right through his business it is anti-our country.'

Again and again footsteps sounded in the passage. They always slowed down outside the door. When the door opened several men slid in silently. They leaned back against the walls to stare.

It went on. 'Who are your friends?'

'I know lots of people. Not many friends.'

'You choose your friends on what basis?'

'Let me think.'

I looked at the faces against the walls as though nothing were there but the walls themselves. He's nerveless, I wanted them to think.

Pairs of eyes punched into blobs of meat. I would not permit myself to decipher more than this.

'Who is your best friend?'

So now we really start. I said nothing.

'Why do you not answer the question?'

The silence went on and on and I folded my arms across my chest.

One of them burst out: 'What is the position with you and the Bantu man?'

I shook my head. I kept my head down and this helped a little. I heard men breathing, that was all. I'm hopeless at contemplation. I thought, how can I shut them out of my mind altogether? But then they all started to leave the room, so I looked up again. Soon I was alone in the room. This astonished me. I anticipated that we had reached the stage at which they lit matches just below your balls.

The sense of freedom went to my head. I moved my chair into a far corner. It was wonderful no longer being in the middle of the room. To steady my hands I sat on them, crushing them against the ridged seat of the chair. When I released them the sight of them fascinated me, mauve and chalky like ancient hands. But they did not shake any more.

The door was unlocked and they brought in a telephone. The security policeman told the detective to connect it to the plug in the skirting board. I gathered that the security policeman was in some way senior, or potentially more menacing, than the detective.

They strolled across to my corner. 'One telephone call only is permitted,' the security policeman said.

'What's the time?' I said.

'This is not important.'

'The person I want to speak to will be in one of two places, depending on the time.'

'The time is about ten-thirty.'

'Thanks.' The telephone was on the floor. They watched me while I dragged two chairs towards it, settled it on one chair and sat down on the other, facing it. The best I could hope for was to put my back to them. I dialled the office number with a discoloured fingernail. After the Johannesburg municipality our switchboard was reputed to be the busiest in the whole of Africa. The eight operators all answered in the same tea-party tone. One could never break it down. Their instructions were to resist these attempts.

Dick's secretary said, 'Hello, Ray, you sound miles away.'

'It's an outside call,' I said.

'He's just going into a meeting, Ray.'

'Please,' I said, 'it's a bit urgent.'

She paused, breathing coolly, determined to impress on me that, despite the tricky decisions she was repeatedly faced with, she never made the wrong one. 'I'll see if I can catch him.'

An indefinite sound came over the line.

'Dick, there's been a bit of a mess-up, I'm afraid.'

'Oh,' he said.

'They'll only let me make one call. I'm at Central Square. Victor's here too. At least I think he is. Dick, can you come round?'

'What on earth are you doing at Central Square?'

'Well. We've been arrested, I suppose you'd say.'

'Why should they arrest you?'

'Dick, they'll be waiting for you at the meeting, and this is a long story, and it'd be easier to explain if you came round.'

'Yes, I do have a meeting,' he said.

'Dick, are you there?'

'They can wait another minute or two.' His voice swerved away as he shared this remark with his secretary and with me. 'Now,' he said to me, 'what is it?'

'I wish I could tell you. But they haven't charged us yet.'

'Where were you arrested and why?'

'At my place. Ours. It's a house in Doornfontein, just a small one, you know the sort. There's been so much on lately I haven't had a chance to tell you. I've left the other house. I'm renting this house in Doornfontein now. We were asleep and they arrived.'

'I don't quite follow. About Victor, I mean.'

'He stays there too,' I said. But why lower your voice? They know it all anyway. They've seen it all too. They've taken possession of our sheets into the bargain. They're probably enjoying listening in on this all the same. Tonight their wives will lap it up, appalled. 'He stayed with me in the other house as well,' I added.

'Rather silly of him, wasn't it?'

'I asked him to. Eventually he agreed. We wanted to be together.'

'Really?'

'Dick?'

'Mmm?'

'I've told them I'm not answering any more of their questions. They must charge us first.'

'Why,' said Dick, 'have you kept us in the dark about yourself and Victor?'

Such a heavy tread behind his words. I was put off my stroke for a moment and said, 'All things considered, it isn't exactly the sort of thing you broadcast to the world, is it?'

'What isn't?'

'What I'm talking about,' I said.

'Which is – what?'

Nothing was going ahead as it should have done. Say if they put a time limit on calls. Three minutes, please. Cut. And so I rushed it. 'I'm sure I needn't tell you I'm not alone here. Not that this matters really. They found us together anyway.'

'I see.'

'But.' What the hell's going on today? I'm not getting through to anybody today. 'Dick, you're not really with me. There's so much I must fill in still.'

'Such as?'

Such as? How does one go on after a cue like that? 'Well, for one thing, now you know why Victor needed that scholarship more than anyone else. It's bad luck, but now he'll have to be dropped from next year's list.'

'By the way. Had he won it, you would have gone with him?'

'Yes. Yes, I suppose so.'

'Odd.'

Odd? 'Okay, I agree with you. But I wish you'd come round here after your meeting.'

'I wonder,' he said, 'if I can be of much help to you before they decide on the charge.'

I don't believe it, I was thinking. But what, precisely, don't I believe?

'I think,' he said, 'I should send someone. Someone who knows the ropes.'

'Who?'

'I will look into it.'

'Will he see Victor too?'

'Without doubt. The two of you.'

'They took Victor away in another van. I haven't seen him since.'

Dick said, 'Our man will assist you, I'm sure.'

It's sunk in now and I don't believe it, I never will.

'Sorry I kept you,' I said.

In another room in the building a not so young man and a young man came very gradually out of chairs. One was a lawyer, a junior partner, I was told later, and the other an articled clerk who took notes from time to time, never at the right time, it seemed to me. They represented the firm retained by the Organisation at all hours of the day and night. The firm specialised, I think, in mining claims and patent rights.

How immaculate the lawyer's outline. I knew the mould well. The younger executives at the Organisation wouldn't have dreamed of coming out of any other, it was wiser not to.

The room was so like the one I had left I began to wonder whether the journey in between the two had actually taken place. Yet it must have done, because I clearly recalled having enjoyed the journey. For one thing, I had noticed sunlight sloping through slatted blinds.

And, how incredible, not a policeman in sight here. I felt my old skin growing over me once more.

I couldn't resist saying to the lawyer, like picking at the crust of an old sore, 'Will Dick be here later?'

'I can't think why he should be.'

I said, 'No, I suppose not.'

If only one could make everything utterly simple, and hate Dick, and be done with it. Instead one was stuck with this awful melancholy.

The lawyer said to me, 'Now, about the bedroom.'

He couldn't overcome his discomfort, never would, I imagine, and he despised me. He could hardly bear to even look at me, I noticed. Perhaps it was for the best, after all, that it was not Dick's face weighted with the same expression ...

I said, 'Can I see Victor Butele now?'

'That is hardly for me to decide.'

'Ask them. You ask them,' I said. 'Tell them I want to see him.'

'This is all beside the point.'

'Have you seen him yet?'

'I am to speak to you first.'

'Where is he?'

'Above us. The ninth floor.' To his articled clerk, 'The ninth, did they say?'

'What have they been doing to him?'

'A few questions. Routine questions, I gather.'

'Couldn't you be wrong?'

The lawyer sighed. Signs of boredom set in round the mouth.

He said, 'The detective in the case has pointed out that there is only one bed in the house, the one in which you and Butele were found. You shared it … regularly … with him?'

My first yes.

'The state of the room made this fairly clear of course. You have lived with Butele in other houses?'

'Just one. Not counting my flat. He only spent weekends there.'

'The previous house was the one in Parkside visited by the detective Prinsloo?'

'So that's his name.'

'I am told so.'

'Yes. He searched it once.'

'At the time he was aware, he says, that something was not quite in order. Possibly extra-legal. He made it his duty to follow up the case. He found it an interesting case, particularly as he was not quite sure where it was leading. For this reason he briefed security branch, who offered assistance. Together, they picked up threads in the townships. Then at Butele's place of work. A disc jockey, I believe? He plays tennis as well?'

The lawyer ordered the articled clerk to pass him some papers. He studied them while we looked on.

'Incidentally,' he said, glancing well above my head, 'there is to be no charge under the Immorality Act.'

I said, 'It's a ridiculous Act anyway.'

'Really?'

'Well, what do you think?'

The lawyer breathed out, started again. 'You will have

realised, of course, that it is our client's interests with which we are concerned. Immediately on being advised of your detention we made certain requests on our client's behalf. Our requests coincided with the State's own view of the matter. The State itself is reluctant to prosecute in a case of this ... nature. You may, if you like, put it down to an agreement reached in the interests of public morals.'

'You mean they're scared?' I said.

'You are not?'

'Don't be stupid, of course I am. But not for the same reasons as the State. Bugger public morality.'

'Nevertheless it exists. Consequently it requires protection.'

'Why did they pick on three in the morning? What do they expect people to be doing at three in the morning – shelling peas?'

'This is an accepted hour in cases of an ... uncertain nature. I thought I had already made it clear. The authorities were not quite sure of the *nature* of the case.'

'You mean home-made bombs in the closet wouldn't have given them quite such a shock?'

Yet another unpleasant smell driven past the lawyer's neatly scoured nostril. 'I am not sure that I understand that question.'

'Talking of questions. You should hear these cops. They're as dumb as their questions.'

'It might interest you to know they all agree they don't care for this case. They call it a dirty case.'

'So would most people. But – sorry. You were talking about your client.'

'I think I should point out that you and Butele could be charged with contravening any number of sections of legislation regulating the residence of Bantu people in urban areas. It has been agreed, however, that this would serve no useful purpose in the circumstances.'

'Just what are the – ' But you mustn't interrupt, you must

listen. For your own good. For both your sakes.

'You consider your relationship with Butele to be a permanent one, more or less?'

'I do. He feels the same. At least, I think he does.'

'From the facts, it would appear so.'

He went on. 'In the circumstances, the State is willing to grant you each permission to leave the country.'

'Passports?'

'No. Exit permits. To be taken up within thirty days.'

'So they *are* scared. You're all shit-scared of us. We might be contagious. We're being kicked out, why don't you say it?'

'I choose not to.'

I bolted. You would have thought I was in my own house the way I ripped open the door, marched down the passage – to where? They were all standing around, interested. I could identify them now. Faces one knew. Years later, possibly, leaving a cinema, waiting for lights to change – I *know* that face. From when, where? I turned round and went back into the room.

'Taking everything into account, I would suggest you are a very fortunate person,' the lawyer said.

'What does your client suggest?'

They were ready to move on, to move up. To Butele, on the ninth floor. The lawyer carried a beautiful softly gleaming briefcase.

'And the State?' I said.

His articled clerk crept up behind him.

'We have accomplished a very great deal for you,' the lawyer said, 'in a very short time.'

'Yes, we'll remember that.'

'You will be released later today. Your only obligation till your departure will be to report to the nearest police station daily. You will appreciate of course that any contact between you and Butele would be undesirable.'

'Until the thirtieth day. What happens to Victor in the meantime?'

'Butele will be taken to the township. Like you, he will report to the police daily.'

Don't let them pity you or laugh at you. 'Happy Christmas,' I said. But I should not have said this. When one is either angry, or afraid, one should shut up. I should have said, if there's anything he wants. Here, take this cash, it's all I've got on me at the moment. And tell him not to forget that place name. Malaga. Remind him we're going to tear it apart in only thirty days' time.

I was alone in the room and it was open to the sky and there was no policeman squatting at the door, at least not yet. Somewhere the sun was setting and the light came and went, I did not know what to do next. I missed my watch and I cursed myself for not begging a cigarette from the lawyer. It occurred to me, then, that neither the lawyer nor his clerk had smoked. They've made up their minds to live to a ripe old age, that's what it is. They know all about themselves and what's going to happen to them. Cancer of the lung is one thing that will not happen to them.

Len Silver. Somehow I must get hold of Len Silver. He must be told he can't help us any more. He's a busy man, he is not the sort of man one should inconvenience. If I had pen and paper I'd start a list immediately. So much to put down on it. One must be practical from now on. Victor – is his vaccination up to date, for instance?

I sat next to the window. The clouds were like hills. Half an hour later they were like countries. I spotted Turkey and the whole of South America. The countries were the colour of putty and the ocean between them was a chilly green. The sun was on the other side of the building, a great continent of cloud must have blotted it out in the meantime. The absence of light at sunset lowers one's spirits. I looked across the city in which yesterday I had been free, though worried. A city of such passionless colours just at this moment. Sand, straw, butterscotch, stone. As I looked out I became frightened again. The day's events washed right up against me in very cold individual waves.

Authority, in police terms, was something new to me, though not to Victor. He had always lived close to it, while I was remote from it. My people conceived authority, and executed it, his people were here simply to obey it. But oh well. Soon it won't matter to us any more. And who knows? Maybe one day, in about a million years' time, neither of us will even bring it up as a subject for serious conversation.

I stretched out my legs and what I caught in the side of my eye was a shadow rather than a shape as it passed by the window and was gone. A great – what? A prehistoric bird, I think. No known bird in the world today is quite that size.

Its wingspan alone must be.

Wingspan? What do you know about wingspan?

There is no light now, so there cannot possibly be a shadow. Yet something cast a sort of shadow across my eye.

I stood at the window and for the first time looked down. Five floors up is too high yet not high enough. You can see the shadow on the pavement but cannot quite make out a single feature of it. It is not a shadow, however, it is a shape. This I do know. I can identify a leg and an arm. Or is it two legs, no arms? The shape is no longer on its own on the pavement. People are drawn to it from all directions in a hurry.

I ran into the passage. A policeman was limping slowly up and down outside the door. I ducked past him and I heard him shouting. I turned a corner into another passage and ran on and came to both a lift and a stairway. I hammered at the lift button, which immediately came to life, glowing red, then I went to the top of the stairs and looked down. I raced back to the lift, where the policeman caught my arm. He was still shouting at me.

I began to kick him and scream at him. Why why? Get a doctor, he isn't dead. Where's the fucking doctor? Fuck you, he isn't dead.

When the lift door opened there were hundreds of them. They gathered round, all chattering at the same time. I tried to force my way through them, using my feet mainly. Several of them held me in the end.

'No,' someone said, 'definitely no.'

'I want to see him,' I said.

'It is undesirable,' they said.

'Just this once,' I said.

'Impossible,' they said.

'In thirty days we'll be gone,' I said.

'The orders are no.'

'We could leave earlier if necessary.'

'You must realise that – '

'Where's that lawyer?' I said.

'What good can a lawyer do?'

'Let me go down. Please,' I said.

'It is not permitted,' they said.

'I want to see him,' I said.

'It will make up a disturbance in the street,' they said.

Funny, I had always been under the impression I had given freedom with my love, but this was not so. It was quite the reverse in fact, and in this way I damaged him. I set him floundering, whereas beforehand he had managed his life pretty well.

I drove him into one corner after the other. He fretted about the cockeyed balance in our relationship. He considered he brought nothing into it, for the reason that he was like a man with his hands cut off. We were in my world. What belonged to his world could not be included, it had to be left behind through force of circumstance.

As long as Victor was close at hand, I felt it possible to carry on with my life in the white world. He was my backing, I felt.

When I was in bed in the upstairs guest room at Frankie's after Victor died I thought, they are all so happy in this house I don't want to leave it.

They made me learn Spanish out of three little books with covers like damp skin. Uno dos tres cuatro cinco seis siete ocho nueve diez once doce trece. Don't try for an accent à la Castellana, they said. It makes them split blood and worse in Andalucía.

Because I could not keep my mind in order at this time I did not have to sign the book at the police station even once. Geoff wrote a report that afterwards we called the magic wand.

Now and then the pills had no punch whatsoever and so Geoff would bring out his needle and how wonderful it was and I wanted the feeling to go on forever.

But I behaved badly when Margaret came. Fresh-old terrors brought on a screaming fit that the neighbours complained about in a crisp note and so she left. Another day Geoff led her up the stairs and she sat down next to the bed in a frilled dress which did not seem right on her. Are people dressing differently now as a sign of some change or other which is being kept from me? I wondered.

She said, 'Please don't think Dick sent me. He wouldn't dream of it, he really has nothing to say. We've never discussed it and I suppose we never will. I knew you must be unhappy and so that's why I'm here.'

At least her brusqueness was still intact and I knew I was warming to her all over again. She said, 'I was almost sure about you two. So, when I was told, it simply fell into place. Perfectly all right.'

As a rule, she never gave a thought to people's sex lives, she said. 'Perhaps one should,' she said.

Kindly write to me, she ordered. She would like us to meet on her next visit to Europe. Where would I be living? she asked.

'Spain. To start with.'

'Cheer up. It's Christmas,' she said.

People say Christmas Day is the hottest day of the year, alternatively it pours with rain. In the garden my obscenely white legs strayed about in the sun. Frankie brought out a Christmas cake with the iced coffee. He cut the cake under a syringa tree.

On the telephone my mother had said, Oh I knew you'd let us down in the end.

I was well rehearsed and I lied immaculately. You lose everything in the end if you don't lie. I lied for all our sakes. I like to think I lied for their sakes rather more than for my own, but how does one know? I had been given the chance of a trip to Europe, I said. Why, how – finally, when? she asked. Tomorrow, I said. Good heavens, she said. I'll write and you must come over soon, let's have fun over there, I said.

It saddened me, even as a child, that, while loving my mother, I had no influence over her.

I had some money still and I gave it to Frankie to send records to Victor's daughter.

In the garden, when the cake had been taken inside out of the heat, I spoke to Geoff, because I would soon be leaving. I did not have to plead with him. He acknowledged that responsibility must be taken on again sooner or later.

He said, 'He has been buried in the township cemetery which looks to me exactly the same as cemeteries anywhere. Some relations turned up at the funeral. Cousins, I think.'

'It's odd,' I said. 'All the time I thought I was saving him. But what I was doing was just the opposite. It's happened before, I suppose.' I rambled on. But it isn't possible to communicate your suffering. You can talk your head off but I don't think there is any way of putting it across to someone else.

I said, 'He had a rough time, one way and another. I think everything would have been all right, though, once we'd got away.'

Geoff said, 'He did it so you would be free. But of course you know that.'

'The thought of living in another country that he had no roots in worried him nearly all the time. He worried that in some way he wouldn't be able to carry it off. Now and then he tried to pretend he wasn't worried and he looked forward to the change. Everything got on top of him and he lost his nerve, that's the only way I can think of it.' In between these lines

163

somewhere lay the truth that one was after.

Frankie questioned Geoff. 'Do you think I'm being too fancy about the Alameda?'

'It's a splendid street.'

'You don't think I've laid it on too thick?'

'Ray will soon know if you have.'

We whisked past a power station in an impossibly neat garden on the airport road. Then came more factories, all of them hissing yellow steam but each one set in its own polished garden. An overhead bridge darkened the car for an instant. In the hard sunlight inside the car I lit cigarettes and passed them round.

My permit would be handed over at the airport. Occasionally in bed I had been aware of comings and goings downstairs in the house. Geoff had dealt with the appropriate people, he brushed it all aside. He would smile over his shoulder as he skimmed out of the room.

I thought of getting a job in London after Spain.

'You'll be there for the first cinerarias,' Frankie said.

He sighed. 'By the time we get there in April they'll look like a lot of broken down lupins. Can't we go over earlier this year?'

'No,' said Geoff, 'we can't.'

We marched into the transit hall with our eyes straight ahead. The detective darted at us from behind a pillar to say, 'Follow me.'

'Why?' said Frankie.

Everyone in sight became transformed into someone in authority. I hesitated, looking. But they all scattered to various counters and only an airport policeman hovered on the outskirts picking at his chin while he looked us over.

They took my airline ticket and my baggage while the detective stood close beside me. The texture of his skin made one think of jelly beans.

'There is this room for you. Follow me,' he said.

'I bet it's a hideous room. Can't we stay here?' Frankie said.

The detective frowned. There was meat all over him, not fibrous, but buttery meat. He was alive, and had put on weight in the past month.

Frankie pointed. 'That stuffed wildebeest over there is so comforting. At least, I assume it's stuffed.'

'You must not speak to anyone,' the detective said.

We settled down on olive green vinyl chairs around a tipsy metal ashtray in the middle of the hall while Geoff went to get coffee. The detective sat nearby and repeatedly glanced at me.

I was only half-doped, Geoff was meticulous about how much and when and why. I kept on reliving the afternoon I lay next to water while Victor played with his daughter out of sight.

'You'll love Oswald,' Frankie said.

I didn't like the name.

The other names to remember were Beatriz and Luis and Jasper and Willy. Beatriz and Luis looked after Geoff's house. They lived in a flat at the back. Jasper and Willy came over from London every winter to stay in the house. Willy was Geoff's cousin and so Geoff did not charge them as high a rent as he could have done. Frankie thought this silly of him. Willy wrote brittle biographies of royal dynasties which were pounced on by the Book of the Month Club as a matter of course. Jasper ran Willy's house. He often spun yarn on a hand-loom.

Oswald lived in his own oak forest near Tarifa from where you looked over the Straits to the low glassy shores of Africa. His other houses were in London and Montreux.

'I've always felt you should meet Oswald,' Frankie said.

He added, 'There's something about a banker.'

Geoff bounded back to the hatch for the third cup.

'This isn't coffee, it's tea,' Frankie said.

He peered into his cup. 'No, it isn't. What *is* it?'

A voice came over in fits and starts. 'Suid-Afrikaanse Lug-diens aankondig die vertrek van sy – '

'I must piss,' I said.

The detective sloped along beside me. Gents. Here. Whites. Blankes. The wiring must have been faulty, the lights flicked on and off flirtatiously.

As though unaware of the footsteps behind me, I let the door fly back on its spring. The detective pressed on, he could not help himself. I stood watching the smoky shape your face makes in tinted tiles.

I piss on the fatherland.

The detective and I had the place to ourselves. Nevertheless he had chosen a bay only one away from me. Nothing was coming out of him. I was finished myself and I listened to the silence. A minute passed, still nothing. The silence boomed with a sense of strain and I was bitterly amused with it all. I glanced sideways at the detective. There it was, a rigid profile, not quite baboonish, that shivered ever so slightly above the bull neck.

I stepped down, facing him. I burst out laughing. Victor would not have approved, he disliked people who showed off. But the dangerous thing about hate is that it seems so reasonable.

I crossed to the basin. Palmolive with streaks like rust. The detective's face came to rest in the mirror. How deathly pale it was. Only the eyes had colour in them, glue-coloured, dabs of snot on the whites.

He shoved my permit towards me without a word and turned aside.

I went ahead into the hall and Frankie was looking past me at the detective and his face showed that he took it all in.

He stood up to breathe out. 'We live in stirring times.'

An airline bag was in my hands.

Passenger Butele absent today. One thing about us, we could never get to the stage of taking it in our stride, as other people do, in time.

In the florist's window the proteas were bound in cones of plastic. Proteas don't sweat, but these ones seemed to want to.

And next door in the bookstall that week's issue of *Rooi Rose*, *Personality*, *Scope*, *Huisgenoot*. But didn't they all have the same face on their covers last week?

We walked on. Cold red arrows showed the way, only a fool could miss it.

'Well, well,' Frankie said. I had never before known him to be at a loss for words.

I walked on and on. I was filled with a curious mixture of adventure and desolation.

'You can start all over again,' Frankie said.